Death Before Dawn

Death Before Dawn

SEAL STRIKE: Book One

Martin L. Strong

Writer's Showcase
New York   Lincoln   Shanghai

Death Before Dawn
SEAL STRIKE: Book One

Writer's Showcase
an imprint of iUniverse, Inc.

For information address:
iUniverse
2021 Pine Lake Road, Suite 100
Lincoln, NE 68512
www.iuniverse.com

ISBN: 0-595-18454-5

Printed in the United States of America

This book is dedicated to the steely-eyed warriors of FOXTROT Platoon, SEAL Team Four and to the brave SEALs who selflessly gave their lives during Operation Just Cause, Republic of Panama, so that others could live in peace and freedom.

I shall be telling this with a sigh
Somewhere ages and ages hence;
Two roads diverged in a wood, and I—
I took the one less traveled by,
And that has made all the difference.

Robert Frost (1916)

PROLOGUE

The rain sliced at sharp angles, mixing easily with the young boy's tears. His hand slowly wiped away both, trembling ever so slightly. The boy didn't seem to mind the chill, unlike the others who were shivering. Matthew Barrett knew better than to show weakness. He'd been raised to act like a man. To ignore trivial distractions such as wind and freezing rain.

Matt's father demanded manliness at all times, a constant state of martial discipline was Matt's personal code of conduct. A code that stood as law in the Barrett household. A code that ruled young Matt's world. Matt continued to stand, silently staring, oblivious of the many raincoat clad mourners. His attention was on the dark muddy hole.

He watched as the rain poured down the sides of the six-foot deep trench containing the sharp outline of his father's casket. Matt stood numbly for what seemed like hours, ignoring the somber proceedings. Struggling to mask his rage and frustration. The baritone voice of the old Episcopalian minister faded in and out of Matt's consciousness.

The rhythm of the driving storm intruded rudely on the old man's eloquent message, the howling wind rising and falling. A marine honor guard, complete with shiny chrome rifles, polished dress shoes and brass fittings, marched slowly into Matt's view. They moved deliberately, finally stopping next to the gravesite. The marine in charge brought the detachment to attention.

The formation was impressive even in the rain. Most of the Barrett family stood within a foot or two of the honor guard. The young marines, eyes locked forward, silently awaited their cue to execute the ceremonial gun salute to a fallen comrade. It didn't matter to these professionals that they had never met the now deceased Colonel Arthur Barrett, United States Marine Corps.

In the great tradition of the corps, any marine, all marines, were marines for life and therefore worthy of a fellow warrior's respect. Because of this, Matt believed the men of the honor guard could be forgiven. Forgiven for not knowing the true nature of the man they honored.

Matt's red eyes scanned the miserable assembly of disjointed humanity. A pitiful collection of idol worshipers and kiss asses, huddled together in a shapeless mass of umbrellas and oversized raincoats. The truth was that Arthur Barrett was the only success story in a family filled with morons and fools. The worthless leeches all fed off his father in their own way, and Matt knew they'd miss his father more than anyone.

The professional wax finish refused to give the probing raindrops the satisfaction of affecting the deep polished look of the dark mahogany coffin. The harder the raindrops struck the wood the higher they bounced. Matt was mesmerized by the effect. The sharp report of the honor guard's rifles made Matt jump, jolting him out of his trance.

He shifted his attention toward the marines as they executed their ceremonial dance in silent unison. Arthur Barrett would have been proud. With the last echoes of the rifle shots drifting away, a tall well-conditioned officer in his early fifties approached Matt's mother and placed a triangle shaped bundle in her lap. The widow looked down at the deep blue field and bright white stars on the flag then shifted her gaze up to the three silver stars resting on each shoulder of the marine general. Their brilliance easily pierced the pouring rain as the senior Marine Corps representative spoke the words heard by generations of patriotic mothers.

"Mrs. Barrett, on behalf of the President of the United States and the men and women of the Marine Corps, a grateful nation presents you with this flag." Matt rode home in silence, squeezed tightly in between his over fed cousin Ralph and his always over perfumed Aunt Celia. The overall effect of sight and smell made him feel queasy. It took forever to travel the relatively short distance from the cemetery back to his house.

When they finally pulled into his driveway Matt didn't hesitate. He jumped out of the rented limousine before it came to a complete stop, bounded up the porch steps two at a time and yanked open the front door. Streaking through the foyer and into the narrow hallway of his two-story brick house, Matt turned a corner and pounded up the carpeted stairs.

Matt stepped inside his bedroom and slammed the door, safe at last in the peaceful seclusion of his rather cluttered sanctuary. The noise of guests arriving downstairs mixed with the metallic clattering of folding chairs as Uncle Billy directed the catering staff.

Matt didn't care. He tossed his body in the air and twirled half way around, landing on his bed in a jumble of legs and arms. Determined to ignore the noise and the people, Matt rolled on his back and took a deep breath. He exhaled slowly, letting his eyes wander across the ceiling.

Matt felt guilty. Not that he really cared that his father was gone now. For a long time Matt had known his father didn't love him. No, that wasn't it at all he realized. Matt felt guilty because his father had cheated him of any chance at redemption. He had robbed him of any opportunity to even up the score and maybe, just maybe measure up to his father's high standards. Arthur Barrett's heavy-handed badgering and strict rules of conduct had driven Matt to tears more times than he could count.

The old man taunted Matt relentlessly. "Don't quit, Matt! Don't let anyone see you cry, Matt! Always be the best, Matt!" On, and on, and on. But no matter how hard he tried Matt was never able to pull it off. Of course now, he never would. Matt understood the full nature of his father's curse and hated him for it. Without his father alive, Matt could never fully measure up. Death had conspired to place the prize beyond his reach. It just wasn't fair! Matt's eyes started to sting again.

Hearing a loud pounding, Matt swiveled his head in a tight arch toward the door. "Go away!" Matt shouted. "I don't want to see anyone!"

"Matt?" The soft feminine voice seemed strangely out of place against the backdrop of the noisy guests downstairs. "Matt honey, can you please open the door?" Matt grudgingly swung his legs off the bed and shuffled to the door. He twisted the knob and eased the door open half way.

Matt could see his mother's outline in the dimly lit hallway. She seemed somehow smaller today and very much alone. Mrs. Barrett looked fondly at her only son. "Matt, please come downstairs and show yourself. People have been asking for you!"

Matt stepped forward and hugged his mom. The hug was tighter and longer than Matt intended, but he felt stronger somehow when they gently pushed away from each other.

Grace Barrett was the product of small town USA. Born and raised in Iowa, her early years were spent helping raise ten siblings. As the oldest, Grace continued to help in the home, until the day she met a handsome, freshly minted marine officer attending school in nearby Sioux City.

Arthur Barrett was ready to take on the world and Matt's mom was swept up by the dashing first lieutenant. Grace needed very little prodding to persuade her to leave home and start her new life. Later in their marriage, when his father's tours to Vietnam started to add up, Matt's mom would draw on her childhood sense of duty to family and muster up the courage to cope.

The love had left the marriage years earlier but his Mom would never think of leaving the colonel. She would never say it, but Matt knew Grace Barrett felt she had been set free by his father's death. "Okay Mom," Matt said, smiling weakly. "Let's go down and pretend to like everyone." Grace smiled. She could see the strength in her son's eyes. Matt was so much like her husband. He had the same all-American look. Wavy blond hair, crystal blue eyes and an infectious grin that belied a keen intellect. But Grace knew her son was very different from his father too. He always suffered his setbacks with poise and humor.

Matt and his mother entered the crowded parlor, walking hand in hand. Within seconds they were surrounded by teary-eyed well wishers. Most of the guests had been stuffing their faces with a passion, acting as if the food was going to be taken away. The mixture of bad breath and the press of so many bodies made Matt ill. He didn't want their pity. And he didn't need their reassurances.

Matt shoved himself away from the crushing weight of the guests, moving toward what looked like the nearest point of escape. Cracking open a solid oak door, Matt slipped quickly into his father's den. It took a moment for his eyes to adjust to the dim interior of the room. He then recognized his terrible mistake.

Standing transfixed, Matt's attention was riveted to a small object across the room. It sat in a special place high on the mantle near the rest of the mementos collected by his father over the years. One thing was for certain; Arthur Barrett had been an achiever of the first order. The walls were covered with splendid plaques and fancy certificates, each by itself worthy of praise and awe. But eventually any visitor to this, the most sacred place in the Barrett home, would see the object on the mantle and stand humbled.

The oak frame was noble in its simplicity. The shadow box was designed to display his father's accumulated military insignia and personal awards. The box was rectangular and topped by a triangular section that held a properly folded American flag. The box was lined in striking Marine Corps red felt. The soft felt provided a startling contrast for the single most powerful object in Matt's young life.

The Congressional Medal of Honor seemed to pulse brightly as if possessing its own internal power source. Matt stared at the medal. The pale blue ribbon was designed to be worn around the neck. If you looked real close you could see little white swirls dancing along its length, twisting and twirling down until the two sections of cloth joined together with a ring made of gold.

Suspended below the ring was the medal itself. Crafted in twenty four-carat gold, it was designed in keeping with the United States Navy's version of the nation's highest award for heroism and courage under fire. Yeah, the old man was a genuine war hero. Turning with great difficulty, he walked to the large oak door and paused before opening it. Matt set his jaw in determination. Somehow, he had to find a way to beat his old man.

CHAPTER ONE

A thousand pieces of broken beach shells worked their jagged edges into Matt's exposed flesh. This wasn't any fun at all, he thought, grimacing in pain. Since graduating from college, Matt's life in the United States Navy had been nothing short of a living hell. The officer recruiter at the University of Nebraska had never indicated things could get this bad. Matt, like everybody else who volunteered for the elite SEAL teams, was sold a bottle of genuine snake oil.

Seduced by images of heroic frogmen defeating America's enemies using only their bare hands, Matt wanted the admiration and respect the Navy's special warriors received. Just being selected for SEAL training was an honor. Matt was determined to make a name for himself in the SEALs. There were plenty of opportunities in the teams to see combat and maybe even pick up a few medals along the way! Matt had it all figured out.

"Damn it!" Matt muttered under his breath, his mind returning violently to the present. Every time he attempted to improve his lot and get more comfortable, the shift in body position only exposed a new patch of his skin to the deadly little shells. Even when he tried to take a short catnap, the tiny slivers of shell woke him like a sadistic alarm clock.

Nearby, seven other dark shapes lay hidden, each suffering their own personal torture. A long white beam of light flitted back and forth like a lazy finger, tracing along the shoreline near Matt and his men. Matt

1

instinctively pressed himself to the ground to reduce his already small silhouette against the sand. The seekers high on the ridge spent an extraordinary amount of time straining to pick out anything amiss on the beach below.

Matt realized the enemy troops weren't in a hurry. The SOBs could park anywhere and pitch camp if they wanted, he thought angrily. He was certain of one thing–his SEALs couldn't advance inland toward their objective until the patrol moved on their merry way. Matt stared at the luminescent face of his dive watch in frustration. He and his men were running out of time. "If the jerks don't move soon, I'm going to fire them up!" Matt whispered quietly. He knew firing at the patrol wouldn't help matters though—no matter how good it might feel to break the stalemate.

Matt and the other men needed to stay put and be patient. The minutes crawled by and Matt's left leg fell completely asleep. Soon after the officer dozed off the enemy patrol departed from the ridge, unseen by the sleeping Lieutenant Junior Grade. Over the next hour Matt drifted in and out of consciousness. His mind wandered freely, drifting as usual to the impact of his decision to join the navy after college.

Part of the reason he joined was to avoid the post college decision to grow up and do something productive with his life. His mother had reacted badly to the news when halfway through college Matt joined the navy recruit officer training candidate program. Grace Barrett didn't see anything positive in her son's involvement with the military. She was even more concerned when Matt told her he'd requested assignment to the SEAL teams.

Matt never shared his mother's reservations. For him it all seemed so natural. From the very beginning he knew in his heart he was doing the right thing. Matt had always been athletic, excelling in many sports throughout high school and college. So it was no surprise to those who knew him when he crushed the SEAL physical screening test on the first attempt. The SEAL instructor administering the test sat Matt down and tried one last time to dissuade him by letting him know the odds of becoming a SEAL.

The SEAL teams routinely screened three to five thousand people a year. The hopeful candidates came from high schools, colleges, the United States Naval academy and even active duty sailors from the fleet. From this population SEAL instructors selected approximately seven hundred and twenty men a year for orders to the six-month long Basic Underwater Demolition SEAL, or BUD/S course in Coronado, California.

As the son of a Medal of Honor recipient Matt's paperwork was destined to fly through the navy bureaucracy, and by the time he graduated from school Matt had his orders for BUD/S in hand. Matt spent some time considering the daunting attrition statistics for the commando school. The seven hundred and twenty students who arrived throughout the year were assigned to six, one hundred and twenty man classes. Traditionally only twenty students from each class finished the six-month long course.

It dawned on Matt as he read his new orders that day, that he might be making a big mistake. But it was too late. Within days Matt was on a plane bound for California. A sharp whistle jerked him awake, and his body tensed up. *Why couldn't these jokers just move on?* He shook his head to clear the cobwebs. As if in answer to his question the security patrol, their voices barely audible above the wind, turned and began marching briskly away from the SEAL's position.

The acronym SEAL stood for sea, air and land. It implied the navy's finest were capable of striking by sea or air while executing special operations missions against high visibility targets ashore. The demands placed on men and equipment operating in this manner was unique. All eight of Matt's men continued to lie motionless for another five minutes, allowing the patrol to get beyond the range of small arms fire.

Matt was the first to move. With a series of deft hand movements he signaled for the team to get up and move toward their objective, the high dominating ridge that separated them from the dense inland terrain. The same ridge earlier occupied by the enemy beach patrol.

The serpentine path in front of them stretched for a hundred yards or more. The SEALs tried to maintain a separation of four to five yards between them. Spacing between patrol members was critical in a small group such as this. Get too close and one burst of machine gun fire or one well-thrown hand grenade could take out half the team. Spread out too far and the silent hand and arm signals would be too difficult to use in the dark.

The camouflaged figures covered a pre-assigned side of the patrol, sweeping their weapons back and forth. The key to this method was to move the eyes in coordination with the movement of the weapon. Most problems would be detected visually. If you were sweeping correctly, no time would elapse between seeing a threat and pressing the trigger to deal with it. The group would patrol in this manner while covering both the left and right fields of fire.

The point man was responsible for looking where they were going. He focused on threats close to the patrol and further out on their path. The rear security maintained coverage of the trail left behind by their passage, a process that resulted in a three hundred and sixty-degree zone of defense around the men.

The patrol was rolling into a natural rhythm. Each SEAL walked in single file stepping gingerly into the footsteps of the man in front. In this way the point man determined the best path for the rest of the group, reducing the possibility of anyone else tripping a booby trap. Matt kept tight control over his team as it glided across the rock-strewn plain. From time to time he couldn't help looking over his shoulder to see if the combat rubber raiding craft still lay hidden in the inky darkness offshore. The sharp barking of a roving dog up ahead froze the painted warriors in mid-step. The patrol waited a few minutes to make sure the dog wasn't barking at them then continued ahead silently.

The little island teemed with insects, rodents and even small foxes, more than enough to justify the actions of the dog. Matt took advantage of the break. He pulled the waterproof UHF radio out of a shallow side pouch on his equipment vest and pressed the rubber coated push-to-talk button. Hissing softly into the tiny microphone, Matt attempted to pass the mission's first event codeword.

"Tango two-nine-one this is tango two-nine actual, codeword PEBBLES, over."

Just outside the natural sea barrier of the reef the black combat rubber raiding craft, or CRRC, bobbed gently as the deep ocean swells passed silently and majestically underneath. In frustration Matt checked his watch then attempted the call again. The radio's batteries were brand new and unused! Why wouldn't they answer?

The sleeping SEAL radioman awoke with a violent jolt, nearly launching him back into the waiting sea. The boat pool leader held the second call and turned expectantly. He pointed at the chattering radio, just in time to see his sleeping radioman regain his balance and composure. The third radio call filled the quiet night air. The boat pool leader snarled at his drowsy radioman and grabbed the handset away from him. He jabbed the push-to-talk button.

Matt started to tear away the heavy layers of waterproof wrapping around the radio to expose the function dials. Maybe the frequency setting was wrong. He rotated the selector switch left–taking it off frequency then returned it to its original position. Matt's fourth attempt was interrupted by the CRRC commander.

"Tango two- nine actual, this is tango one-one, say again your last, over."

Matt waited impatiently until the call was completed before responding in a clear and hostile voice.

"PEBBLES, PEBBLES, I say again! PEBBLES, over!"

The boat pool leader recognized the tone immediately and tried to make his brief answer appear apologetic.

"Roger your last. Good luck. Tango one out!"

Matt shoved the UHF radio back in its pouch and snapped it shut. Those bastards were asleep! He twisted around to face the lanky point man squatting next to him.

"Let's get the show on the road, Duke, we're burning moonlight!"

Duke's slow nod of affirmation was lost in the darkness but his body language signaled acknowledgment of the order. The point man stood up easily, heading once again toward the high ridge above. The small team crept silently up the steep embankment, their eyes trying to pierce the darkness. Duke reached the edge ten minutes later.

The point man could clearly see the coastal road winding across their intended path like a gray ribbon. He glanced toward his left to the spot where the enemy patrol had searched. He watched their bobbing flash-lights disappearing in the distance as they rounded a rocky bend two hundred yards down the shoreline.

Duke raised an open hand to signal to Matt and the others his intention to advance. Knees creaking and snapping in protest under the heavy combat loads, the team rose up and continued their tense movement, following Duke once again. With great stealth the group of young warriors passed over the top of the ridge.

Duke quickened the pace a little until he reached the coastal road. He stopped at the road's gravel boundary and carefully sank down to his belly. Twisting back around with excruciating slowness, he used his hand and made a slicing motion across his throat to signify to the rest of the team that a danger area blocked their path of intended travel. Duke added a second hand signal resembling a peace sign. This designated the road crossing as a level-two threat.

The alert point man's signals indicated a situation that required very special handling. In accordance with the team's standard operating procedures or SOPs, each SEAL in turn passed Duke's signal back until the rear security acknowledged with a thumbs up. Matt allowed time for this process before passing his command to execute the proper tactical drill. The command was again repeated down the patrol. The SEALs rapidly advanced to the gravel road, each in turn stopping in front of Matt. They peeled off left and right at the LTJG's direction until the entire team was deployed around him in a defensive perimeter.

The SEAL enlisted men were keenly aware they'd fallen behind the planned timetable. Each looked expectantly at their young officer to catch a hint of what he was going to do. Matt squatted, balancing evenly on the balls of his toes while he weighed his options. Standard SEAL team operating procedures for a level two threat area called for placement of his most powerful weapons, M-60 machine guns in this case, on either flank of the road crossing, the big belt fed guns effectively covering either approach.

With the men deployed, Duke began his movement across the road reinforced by a grenadier carrying an M-203 grenade launcher strapped under his M-16 rifle. Once across, the triangular formation formed by Duke at point and the two machine gunners on the flanks ensured the team could adequately deal with any worst-case contact scenarios. Matt's real problem now was time.

The SOP book didn't cover how to balance threat level against time line considerations. This was a command decision and as the officer in charge he was expected to figure it out himself. As the guys would say, that's why Matt was paid the big bucks. With the full weight of the decision on his shoulders, Matt began to panic.

The dark night hid many mysteries for the young warriors. The wide-open terrain and dominating high ridge placed the SEALs in a terrible position.

Duke stared nervously at the opposite side of the road. He knew it wasn't a good idea to screw around exposed where they were. There wasn't so much as a bush to hide behind here on the roadside. Duke took a long look around. Any minute he fully expected to hear the enemy patrol returning, crunching down the ridgeline behind them, effectively cutting them off from the rubber boats offshore.

Matt watched his point man. Watched as the two-man point element went to ground on the far side of the road. He signaled for the rest of the team to move out and execute the main crossing. Duke looked back until he saw the rest of the team start to move. Only the whites of his eyes were visible on his painted war face.

"They're moving across!" he hissed at his partner.

Duke moved forward a few more yards to create enough space for the arriving team members. He returned his attention to the wide, open area awaiting the SEALs. Then Duke froze. He heard the distinctive sound of a rifle's selector switch clicking to the automatic fire position. Duke screamed a warning as he thumbed his weapon's safety and opened fire.

"Contact front!" he shouted.

Caught in mid-stride on the gravel road, the other SEALs could not open fire without hitting their own men. The first four team members thundered across the road and threw themselves onto the ground next to Duke. Unfortunately the rest of the SEALs following closely behind had no room to lie down, causing them to stand in place for a moment right in the middle of the road.

Matt and the rear security were still lying on the ground between the two machine gunners. They couldn't see past the pileup in the road. Nor could they return fire without shooting into their fellow SEALs. Matt stared in disbelief at the dark huddle. Damn it! This was ridiculous! Matt jumped to his feet screaming at the clustered SEALs.

"Move it! Get across the road and hit the deck!" Matt's words cut through the noise and spurred the men to action.

Matt gestured for the machine gunners to also cross. Before Matt had a chance to join the team on the opposite side of the road, he was knocked to the ground by a deafening explosion. Blazing red tracers angrily stitched across the night sky on both flanks and directly over the heads of the surprised SEALs. The intense fire was coming from a heavy machine gun well positioned on a low hill directly to their front. Matt's team got their act together and crawled online, coming up on either side of Duke and the now wounded grenadier.

The SEALs kicked into high gear, returning deadly coordinated fire. Commands and questions were shouted by the men in cool, measured reaction to the enemy contact. Their training had taken over. The men were on autopilot now.

But Matt and his rear security man still lay flat on the roadbed, stunned into silence and inactivity by the fierce attack raging all around them. His numb mind struggled in slow motion to grasp what was being played out all around him in all too vivid detail. He was vaguely aware that his men were returning fire. He needed to snap out of his mental fog. Matt was aware that a real disaster was unfolding in front of his eyes.

Despite his men's initial reaction, the enemy was in command of the engagement. Pounding them from well-prepared positions on higher ground. Matt was regaining control. He ran through his list of choices discarding all but one. Matt shook it off and crawled up behind Duke. It was time to get a grip on the situation.

Matt's first command to consolidate their forces was drowned out by the intense enemy fire. From their current location any attempt to win by firepower alone was doomed. The SEALs position was lower than the enemy's firing point. It was nearly impossible for bullets to stop and drop into prepared pits. Matt knew what had to be done, and screamed out the order.

"Consolidate!" Matt needed to pull the squads together before maneuvering toward the attackers above them.

The SEALs heard the LTJG this time and moved on their bellies until they were assembled in a tightly organized skirmish line. Scanning the surrounding terrain, Matt spotted a deep ravine thirty yards off to their right. He needed to get the guys out of this kill zone. If they could make it to the ravine, they stood a fighting chance of surviving this mess.

The boat pool leader offshore heard the abrupt explosion of small arms fire and knew it meant trouble. From his vantage point, tracers streaked across the night like a surreal display on the Fourth of July. He quickly assessed the men in the boats were safe enough for now. The boat pool leader reached under his combat vest and brought out a night vision scope. He needed to know what was happening inland!

He turned the device on and focused on the area of the firefight. It looked like all the shooting was taking place high above the insertion beach.

"Well, what's up, Jake? Can you see our guys?" asked one of the boat crew.

Jake did his best to describe the action. "I guess the boys made it off the beach all right. But they stepped into it near the coast road. As long as the tracers continue to head out to sea I figure they'll keep getting hit hard. I just hope nobody puts up an illumination rocket. We'll be sitting ducks out here."

Matt ducked to avoid a direct burst of tracers flying right over his head. He'd spotted a way out of the kill zone. He gave the order for the second squad to get up and execute a leapfrog movement to the ravine. However, his command was drowned out as two dark green military trucks roared through the darkness on the team's exposed left flank.

Fire erupted from the vehicle as it careened down the gravel road toward the SEALs. Matt choked off his order and opened fire at the trucks. His men on the left flank automatically shifted their bodies around to engage the newcomers. The patrol now formed a L-shaped firing line. The SEALs were running out of time and ammunition!

The approaching trucks spun sideways and stopped close enough to spray road gravel on the trapped SEALs. Troops poured out, deploying to form a second firing line on the SEALs left flank. The troops immediately opened fire, placing the navy commandos in a deadly crossfire.

Matt's mind screamed in frustration. There was no way they could get to the ravine now. The only option left to them was to assault forward and try to silence the machine guns positioned on the hill. If those guns were taken out the team might survive this action. They could control the high ground and stand a chance of fending off any follow-on attacks. Perhaps then, Matt hoped, he could fight a rear guard action and move rapidly into the island's interior.

Once the SEALs broke contact, Matt would direct the CRRCs to shift to the Western beach to support his team's emergency extraction. Matt jumped to his feet.

"Attack the hill, attack the damn hill!"

The SEALs didn't need any more encouragement. The team understood his intent and began racing uphill toward the chattering guns on the rocky knoll above. In a series of short leap frog movements, the SEALs started to close the distance to their new objective. Their well-conditioned legs pumped hard to keep up the rhythm of the assault drill. Matt continued to belt out commands in sharp clear tones, his earlier confusion all but forgotten. They were doing it!

His men realized collectively that they were better than the enemy. They knew how to fight, and win! Matt didn't have a doubt in his mind they would prevail. Matt's attention was focused forward so he didn't see the men who poured out of the two trucks behind him on the road. The new arrivals moved rapidly to strike the SEALs from behind. Although the force could have overtaken the commandos, they seemed curiously content to keep their distance while following them across the open plain toward the machine gun position.

Matt was reveling in the glory of his assault. He glanced quickly at the second fire team as his team leapfrogged past their position. He'd never been prouder of his men. They were magnificent! Matt gave the order for his maneuvering fire team to hit the ground.

"Everybody down!" he shouted.

As Matt hit the ground, he spotted a flicker of movement off to his right. The spider traps had been well hidden and placed perfectly to cover the slope leading up to the Knoll. Seven riflemen popped up and out of the ground from what had been flat empty terrain. The thin ply-wood covering the spider holes flipped back behind them.

The enemy marksmen poured withering fire into the right flank of the tired men. At the same time, the group following them from the road below threw themselves to the ground and began to select and shoot individual SEALs.

The stunned and beleaguered team had been lured into a perfect three-sided killing zone! The high piercing sound of the ceasefire whistle confused the young LTJG. His mind raced frantically to grasp its meaning. The answer came quickly enough in the shape of a bullhorn; it's rude bellowing intruding on the small arms noise.

"Cease fire! Cease-fire! Clear, and safe all weapons!"

The defeated and thoroughly dead SEAL trainees did not hesitate to comply with the shouted command. Within seconds the once proud commando patrol was organized into two ranks of shivering twenty year olds. The first instructor on the scene growled at Matt and the young officer immediately responded. He hit the ground in a classic pushup position. The rest of the SEAL trainees followed suit. They were required to do so because Matt was their officer in charge.

Matt shouted, "Ready!"

He pressed his body smoothly up and down while maintaining the count. He moved slowly enough for the group of SEAL trainees to keep pace. Matt finished the standard set of fifty pushups and sounded off.

"Hoo-ya, instructor Jackson!"

When the angry instructor directed him to repeat the punishment, Matt knew it was going to be a long training debrief. The SEAL instructors who made up the various attacking "enemy" units wandered back to where the four-wheel drive trucks were parked. Another instructor went to the shoreline to signal the student boat pool to come into the beach for the debriefing.

Matt and his fellow BUD/S trainees were still in the pushup position waiting for permission to stand up.

"Didn't seem quite fair out there now did it, sir?" quipped one smiling instructor.

Matt looked directly into the instructor's eyes, his unspoken opinion clearly etched on his face. The instructor continued to taunt him.

"You know this shit ain't supposed to be fair, sir, just realistic. If you can't pull it off here, in a simple training environment, then you can't pull it off for real!"

Matt lowered his head and stared at the ground below him. His arms were starting to shake violently from the strain.

"It doesn't matter anyway, sir. You guys are so screwed up I personally think you should strip off those fancy ninja clothes and spend some time out in the cold surf zone! That should give you time to think about which ship you'll be assigned to when we kick your asses out of the program!"

Matt could hear the commotion near the trucks indicating the boat pool had arrived. The students in the boat group were spared the pushups as they struggled to load the rubber boats into one of the pickup trucks. The senior instructor overheard the threat to send Matt and the trainees out into the surf zone. He walked over to the group of shaking men. His demeanor was serious.

"We don't have time for any reindeer games!"

The other instructors drifted away. The senior instructor now turned his attention to the class.

"You gentlemen just completed your last student mission in

BUD/s training. After graduation two days from now you will all be shipping out to your first SEAL team. I can assure you lads of one thing. If you screw up in a real world firefight like you screwed up tonight, you won't have to worry about doing pushups! Because you'll be coming home in a body bag!"

Before leaving, the senior instructor looked directly at Matt. His whole body was quivering under the stress of maintaining a perfect pushup posture.

"Sir, wasn't your old man a marine officer?" Matt nodded but did not make eye contact.

"I understand he also won the big blue, is that so?" Matt nodded a second time. He knew where this was going. Even in college people always seemed to find out about his father. Matt's dad was no less than a national hero.

"Well sir, after watching you operate out here I've only got one question. Are you sure you're not adopted?"

The other BUD/S instructors were still close enough to overhear the joke. Laughter echoed off the surrounding hills as the senior instructor walked away in disgust.

"Recover and get off your face, Mr. Barrett. Get your shit picked up and have your people load the trucks."

As he stood up Matt could still hear the laughter of the instructors in his mind. Some heroic leader he turned out to be! No matter how hard he tried he was unable to overcome the fact that he would never measure up to the old man. A man who'd successfully led men in combat, real combat.

His old man had brought most of his men home after their tour of duty. In contrast to Matt who had barely passed the most basic of leadership tests offered in the SEAL course. Although he knew this was only an exercise, Matt was painfully aware he wasn't cutting it as a leader.

Matt would soon be promoted to full Lieutenant upon arrival at his new SEAL command. Failure there would result in disgrace and expulsion from the SEALs. Matt wasn't sure he had it in him to make that final cut.

CHAPTER TWO

2200 Hours–Cairo Egypt

The explosion lit up the night sky in a kaleidoscope of brilliant color. An ear-shattering roar reverberated against the nearby cluster of white stucco upper class homes, violently waking their well-to-do occupants. The terrorists had once again struck at the heart of wealth and influence in Cairo. Their message was clear, no one was safe anywhere. The inept Egyptian government could not protect them.

With one quick stroke the nameless killers snuffed out the useless lives of two decadent infidels and at the same time ignited the flame of hope and freedom for the faceless millions of poor true believers in Egypt. The five men raced through courtyard and out toward the main entrance. A security team reacting to the carnage sprinted through the gate and right into the terrorists.

The lead security man brought his automatic rifle up and pulled the trigger. The weapon didn't fire. To late he realized for the sake of safety, the guards were not locked and loaded. Two AK-47 rounds blasted the thoughts from his mind, striking him in the upper chest. His body flew back into the following group of guards. Two other guards dropped to a knee in a futile attempt to chamber a round. The terrorists dispatched the remaining guards with a fury of automatic fire. To an observer the terrorists appeared to simply run through the security team without slowing down.

Two blocks away a green utility truck flashed it's headlights. The hit team ran down the street without encountering further interference. Sirens began wailing all over the city. The five men dove into the truck and slammed the double doors shut. The green truck pulled away slowly.

The target, the personal residence of Egypt's newly elected president, fell into itself as the weight of the structure overcame the melting support beams. Ten minutes after the attack, the stately home was reduced to a pile of smoking rubble, the polished white stucco stained by the billowing smoke. Somewhere in the ruins lay the bodies of the president and his family. By morning the entire world would hear of this bold strike. The region would hear their message of faith expressed as vengeance as the soldiers of the jihad spread the word of Allah throughout first Egypt and then the Middle East.

The new leader, Mustafa Hammet, was Egypt's last chance at reconciliation and peace. Elected by more than two thirds of the popular vote, he'd been viewed by knowledgeable observers inside and outside Egypt, as a welcome centrist who would comfortably adopt moral rules of national conduct, while focusing on the less fortunate. He'd also sent a message of inclusion to the conservative religious extremists, or holy warriors of Allah. Attempting to bring them into an honest and constructive dialogue with the new government.

Hammet's mandate from the voters had been clear. Accept the social demands of the faithful, but not at the cost of dragging the country back to the Dark Ages like was done in Iran. But the new president never had a chance to try. His violent death on this night was unmistakable testimony to the focused and uncompromising agenda of the radical terrorists. There was no room for compromise or political bargaining. Who now would take up the banner of peace and moderation?

0700 NATO Headquarters–Brussels Belgium

The staff duty officer rubbed his aching red eyes with his palms in a slow circular motion. He would be up all night responding to field reports from NATO forces deployed on peacekeeping missions around the world. As usual the continuous cat and mouse activity expected in disputed areas demanded that the NATO forces supporting the various United Nations resolutions, react to probable worst case scenarios and investigate everything.

Ever since the end of the Cold War NATO had been slowly pulled into events and conflicts defined more by the U.N. Security Council in New York than the NATO headquarters command. The officer yearned for the good old days when the Soviets were clearly the bad guys and NATO the good guys. Even as the Serbs began the tense peace in the former Yugoslavia, NATO was directing its southern commander stationed in Naples to begin contingency planning for a possible NATO intervention in Egypt.

Egypt of all places! Since when did Egypt fall into the NATO threat horizon? Heavy footsteps echoing down the access tunnel signaled the end of his watch. Let someone else get a headache trying to figure it out. He for one was ready to let the rest of the world take a flying leap.

Hagada, Egypt

The Egyptian sergeant froze as movement off to his left caught his attention. His post outside the American military support facility faced the street thus affording him a broad field of view. The movement came from just beyond the soft yellow halo cast on the ground fifty meters down the wall by an overhead security light. He was a veteran of the 1973 Arab-Israeli war and therefore a survivor of the disgrace in the

Sinai. That had been some time ago, but the sergeant had learned hard lessons during that war.

His instincts told him something was not quite right. It had been five months since the first major terrorist bombing attack in Cairo killed the new president. Since then several foreign offices had been bombed and in one case an Egyptian army security patrol had been ambushed. The sergeant shook his head. What did he have to worry about? The Sons of Allah were mad at the Egyptian government, not the Americans.

The sergeant relaxed, regaining his professional composure. He hated pulling double duty, watching the American compound after working all day at his regular assignments. His miserable wife didn't understand the soldier's life. She expected him to make the right friends and then bribe or beg his way out of the long night duty.

Sometimes He thought she might have a point. Quite frankly he didn't understand why the Egyptian Army was spread all over the country protecting foreigners when the troops could be put to much better use hunting down the religious fanatics. Or better yet, taking time off to spend with their neglected families.

From his viewpoint the jihad made no sense at all. These disturbed young men who, through their mad acts of violence, threatened to pull all of Egypt down in flames. His thoughts were interrupted as a small white Volvo sedan turned onto the main street. He watched intently as the vehicle approached his post, a plush hotel leased by the United States Navy and used as a fleet communications support facility. The sergeant's attention was fixed on the driver's face, as the car, a battered looking thing, rolled to a stop directly in front of him.

The driver was a very pretty Egyptian woman in western dress. Her shirt was flimsy and open down to her bra, very risky attire considering the weirdo's and religious zealots roaming about. His eyes scanned the woman's chest with barely disguised admiration. Ah, if only the sergeant had been a few years younger! The woman ignored him. She was busy fumbling with a stubborn city map, attempting to fold it into a neat square. The sergeant could see the stress etched in the pretty woman's face as she finally conquered the document and tried to decipher it in the dim light shed by the hotel sign. The sergeant scratched his head. Tourists were rare here in Hagada and it was really very late. And this one appeared to be a lost little lamb.

Chuckling to himself, the sergeant shrugged and stepped closer to the driver's side of the car. The woman looked up, her face spreading into a brilliant smile. The sergeant bent over to look inside, leaning on the Volvo's hood. He watched in curiosity as the pretty tourist slid her hand out from beneath the open map, his eyes sneaking a peak down her rather impressive cleavage. The old veteran's last thoughts were of his children as three down loaded nine millimeter bullets passed through his forehead, exploding through the back of his skull with a dull popping sound.

The map used by the assassin to conceal the short automatic pistol and six-inch silencer was discolored by a misty cloud of blood. Only the mechanical clicking of the slide and the muffled crash of the sergeant's lifeless body disturbed the peaceful night. He didn't see the Volvo's headlights flashing their silent signal. The lights flashed twice, paused and flashed once more.

Twenty meters away ten darkly clad men appeared from around the corner of a nearby storefront. The team sprinted toward the hotel's entrance. For a split second the group was illuminated by the streetlight, revealing automatic weapons and haversacks filled with explosives. One figure paused to place a round into the bright streetlight in front of the American facility. His suppressed MP-5 SD submachine gun coughed once, plunging the entrance into darkness.

The Volvo pulled away from the curb and rolled slowly toward the bright lights of the other major hotels nearby. The ten-man team sprinted across the front lawn and through the main door of the building. Muffled shots and the sounds of furniture crashing signaled that their pre-rehearsed ballet of terror had begun. The well-trained men set about their bloody night's work with machine-like precision. The few Americans on duty were taken completely by surprise. There would be no survivors.

SEAL Delivery Vehicle Team Two–Little Creek, Virginia

Wham! The sound of the unexpected impact startled Matt. He frantically barked out course corrections to his diving partner into the microphone of his full-face mask. "Come left, come hard left!" The pilot of the SEAL delivery vehicle, or SDV, responded to Matt's frantic commands by deftly adjusting the course of the twelve-foot long mini-submarine.

Matt screamed into the microphone again as the SDV slammed into another underwater obstacle. A row of wooden posts making up the support structure of a harbor pier. As the navigator on this dive, Matt was responsible for detecting objects in the mini-sub's path using the underwater vehicle's sophisticated sonar system.

The navy submersible was shaped like a cigar. The vehicle was fully flooded during underwater operations, requiring the men flying it to wear protective wet suits. The pilot and navigator sat side by side in a cockpit, their low light displays arrayed in front of them. The pair "flew" the SDV above the bottom of the ocean.

This distance was measured in "altitude." The distance below the ocean's surface was measured in feet of depth.

If Matt did his job well, the SDV would be cleanly navigated through unobstructed water to its destination, usually a shallow water target. "Better slide back the canopy and check out the damage, sir!" recommended Pete. Pete was Matt's pilot for today's dive. He was a second class Yeoman. Few people knew that navy ratings and SEAL work were not compatible. All SEAL enlisted men were required to "strike" for a standard job rating. However, only Corpsman, the navy's version of an army medic, actually ever used their navy rating while performing their duties as a SEAL.

Pete slowed the mini-sub down to a snail's crawl. Matt did not miss the edge in his pilot's voice. His enlisted pilot was only twenty years old, a new guy to the teams and still wet behind the ears. But Matt had come to realize during the tough four month advanced SDV operator course, or AOT, that flying the SDV was an art requiring precious little SEAL experience to master.

The really great pilots and navigators just sort of evolved with time and training. Matt was one of those who had not evolved as an SDV artist. The way things were going today he'd be lucky to graduate after this final dive of the course. Thus far, except for Matt's stellar contribution—guiding the SDV directly into a pier at high speed, the kid next to him had nearly controlled the entire dive from the pilot's seat.

Matt slid the canopy door backwards on its track. The SDV had slowed enough for him to stretch his body out of the cockpit so he could inspect the damage. Matt returned to the cockpit and snapped his communications lead back into the SDV's control console. "Sorry Pete. The starboard bow plane is gone!" Matt said.

"That's okay, sir," the kid answered back cheerfully. "I won't tell anybody if you don't! Just reach around behind me and grab the extra bow plane I brought along just in case."

Matt smiled and shook his head in disbelief. "Why did you do that?" he said.

"Well sir, I've had to dive with you for sixteen weeks now. I just estimated how bad things could get with you in here and planned accordingly."

Matt stared hard at his dive partner. The kid was right. After all, Matt truly sucked as an SDV navigator. Matt reached around the Pilot and pulled out the extra bow plane. He leaned out and quickly replaced the critical part of the mini-sub's steering system. "Hey Pete, can we keep this little incident between us?" Matt asked, sliding back into position next to his pilot.

"You know the deal, LT. Whatever happens underwater, stays underwater."

Matt smiled. "Thanks Pete."

"No problem sir. Now close the damn canopy so we can get on with this dive!" Matt didn't answer. He was too busy following Pete's order.

The rest of the AOT class scampered about the pier area as the SDV broke the surface. Matt and Pete had finished their final dive. As always in the SEAL teams, everybody pitched in to get the job done. The entire class scrambled to help lift the mini-sub out of the water and onto the waiting SDV trailer.

Matt and Pete disconnected their communications leads and pulled off their full-face masks, both gulping down real air for the first time in seven hours. He glanced up as somebody shouted down from the quay wall above. "The crane's hooked up, guys. Any time you are ready is all right with us."

Matt and Pete pulled themselves out of the SDV and began the short swim to the quay wall. Behind them the crane was already lifting the jet-black mini-sub out of the water. Another head peaked down at them from the top of the quay wall. "So, how'd it go—you guys?"

Matt was pulling himself up the ladder at the base of the stairs. Pete was still struggling to remove his fins. Both stopped to look at each other before answering. The target had been hit successfully and nobody detected the SDV. In the SEAL teams the standard statute of limitations regarding what really happened on a training mission was six months, another great SEAL rule of thumb. The kid grinned back at Matt in silent understanding. Looking up he shouted. "No sweat! It was a piece of cake!"

Matt pulled himself over the top of the quay wall. He could see the commanding officer, Captain Richards, observing the ongoing SDV lift operation. The captain's eyes reflected the pride he had in his men, even these men, so new to the SDV business. Matt approached the captain staggering under more than one hundred and fifty pounds of mission gear and life support equipment. Next to the captain stood a stocky lieutenant commander, upset about something.

Captain Richards stepped forward, smiling. He extended his hand to Matt. "Well done, lieutenant!" The captain's grip was firm and somewhat painful. Matt's hands were swollen, made soft by the long dive.

"Thank you, skipper," he returned. "My pilot, Petty Officer Pete Simms, completed the operation despite my interference." The captain chuckled and nodded in the direction of the young pilot who had just climbed over the wall.

"Well I'm sure it went well, maybe in a few months or so you'll share the real story with me!" The twinkle in his eye bore witness to the fact that all SEALS were operators first and operators always knew the deal.

"Hey Barrett, I'd like you to meet your new boss." Pete took this as his cue to get away from the brass. Matt nodded one more time to his pilot before turning his attention to the officer in front of him. "Say hello to Lieutenant Commander Sandoval, commander of Task Unit XRAY."

Matt reached out to shake the LCDR's hand. Sandoval still wore a curious "somebody's shit in my corn flakes", look on his face. For some reason he just wasn't having a sun shiny day.

"Pleased to meet you sir," Matt said. The dry polite greeting implied neutrality between two unknown professionals. Sandoval returned the handshake.

"I hear you can't fly an SDV for shit, lieutenant," his dark eyes mocking Matt. His hand stopped pumping abruptly and pulled away.

Matt searched the senior officer's face for some indication he was just messing around. But what he saw instead began to piss him off. "Well sir," Matt began, trying to change the mood of the moment. "I don't think I'll ever win any points for style–that's for sure!" Matt's attempt at charm didn't work. Sandoval snorted.

Captain Richards chuckled, more to change the atmosphere than as a reaction to Matt's comment. "Well I don't think you'll have to worry about that anymore, Lieutenant, because you are being assigned to Task Unit XRAY as the reconnaissance platoon commander. I imagine my SDV's will be safe from damage with you away playing sneak and peek." The captain continued. "Task Unit XRAY's almost finished with her pre-deployment training work up. But with your positive attitude, Matt, I'm sure you can catch up."

Matt stared at Captain Richards in disbelief. The navy personnel bureau had explained to him it would take over a year for an officer to qualify in all the unique SDV related skills. Only then would a new LT be allowed to start the SDV Task Unit training program. The captain's comment indicated Matt would be operational right away.

Matt looked at LCDR Sandoval. "Thank you, sir, I won't let you down!"

Sandoval scowled. "Don't thank me, Barrett! It wasn't my idea! I'm still not convinced you can make the grade so soon out of BUD/S. Nor am I convinced you can make up for missing so much of the standard pre-deployment training."

Matt's initial euphoria over being assigned to the task unit was fading rapidly. This guy was beginning to look like a grade-A jerk. SEAL or not, even a great job like leading the reconnaissance platoon could get shitty if the boss was out to prove a point. And Lieutenant Commander Sandoval, was definitely laying the ground rules for a challenge.

Government House–Cairo, Egypt

The chatter of machine gun fire echoed down the long marble corridor leading into the presidential audience chamber. The new acting president and his immediate family were tucked away in a small side room. Twelve hand-picked Egyptian army commandos guarded the entrance, each willing to lay down his life for the new president.

Fifty feet away, twelve additional commandos stood near the end of the corridor waiting for the attackers to complete their assault of the lower level. The soldiers knew that the political decision had been made already. The Egyptian army commander had refused to throw in his lot with the rebellious government factions led by the religious fanatic Banadar.

Banadar the Faithful, as his followers called him, had grossly miscalculated his ability to influence the Egyptian armed forces. Although most of the air force and navy supported him, in a land of thankless desert and sprawling urban jungle, it was the army that held all the cards. Only hours ago Banadar had been forced to assassinate the stubborn army chief-of-staff. Now he had control of all the army units in and around the city.

Under Banadar's direction the ring of armored personnel carriers and tanks closed in around the government house and presidential offices. Inside the presidential palace the lightly armed fanatics charged up the spiral staircase leading to where twelve stone faced professionals calmly awaited their inevitable fate.

Headquarters NATO Southern Command, Naples, Italy

Admiral Carden pressed the mute button on the TV remote, silencing the CNN announcer for the time being. The coup attempt had been defeated in Egypt. U.S. air power deployed from the aircraft carrier, USS Theodore Roosevelt, had kept the Egyptian air force grounded and ineffective. Egyptian army forces still loyal to the president had defied orders to stay in barracks confinement. Reaching the

palace, they had successfully driven off the lightly armed vehicles surrounding the building.

The president's personal bodyguard had survived their heroic stand
within the palace, defeating the terrorists even before outside help
arrived. United States citizens in Egypt were on alert to evacuate if the
situation deteriorated any further. The fledgling Egyptian government
calmly announced, via the state radio channel, that the situation had
been stabilized.

Admiral Carden stood up and stiffly paced about the room.
Stabilized! What a stupid thing to tell the people. Egypt was anything
but stabilized. The admiral spent hours each day reading reams of intelligence analysis and what he read indicated chaos in the making, not
stability. "You know that bastard Banadar nearly pulled it off," he mumbled half out loud. A communications sergeant nearby looked at him
quizzically. And next time he won't screw up, the admiral thought. The
next time he'd be ready for whatever happens.

Admiral Carden looked around the sixth fleet command and control
center to see if anyone other than the sergeant was near enough to overhear his profane rambling. As the man in charge of the U.S. Sixth Fleet,
and NATO southern commander, he was responsible for providing the
national command authority, the president, national security agency,
and Joint Chiefs of Staff as well as NATO high command, with a quick
assessment of any crisis situation and his recommended plan of action.

The problem in Egypt was quite simple. Protect the current regime
and continue the status quo, or sit on the sidelines, a neutral observer
waiting to make friends with the new government. Another fly in the
buttermilk was NATO's insistence this was not their affair. After stretching their mandate to protect Western Europe by invading Bosnia, and
then Serbia, NATO was wary of moving even further south. If they
stonewalled, the United States may be forced to act alone to save Egypt's
democracy.

But that wasn't a given either. Lately the American president appeared confused about the proper U.S. role in the world. The voters back home wanted the police actions to stop. Morale in the military was sinking due to constant deployment demands. The president himself had compounded the problem by dramatically reducing the size of the American armed forces during his first term in office, and then over committing the forces worldwide in his second term.

Admiral Carden had another, more pressing issue to deal with. His greatest concern was the safety of U.S. citizens living in Egypt. As usual the State Department warnings to leave Egypt were only mildly effective. If a NEO, or non-combatant evacuation operation, was needed to safeguard American lives he would be responsible for making it happen.

His other deep concern was for the men and women in uniform who would bear the cost in blood if things got messy. The admiral walked back to the low table where the phone lines were set up. Placing the receiver against his ear, he dialed with determination.

Time to wake up the idea department and get things down on paper. He finished punching out the number to his operations and plans officer four floors below.

CHAPTER THREE

Isolation Complex–Fort Eustis Virginia

A door slammed somewhere in the dark aircraft hangar. Matt's eyes shot wide open. Damn it! Only minutes had gone by since he'd hit the sack. After planning and rehearsing all day, Matt was dog-ass tired. The mission was complex, requiring several different transportation platforms and a multi-tiered command structure. The rehearsal oversight was becoming a major pain in the ass. Try as he might, Matt couldn't keep the prying senior officers off the backs of his SEALs.

Day after day, the men of Matt's recon platoon poured over the intelligence material related to the target and the environment surrounding the target. Physical training, or PT, was conducted every morning to keep his men strong and hard. The early morning sweat drills also served to increase morale and mission focus. The good-natured banter between Matt's men was at times sharp and biting. The deal was, if you couldn't stand the abuse, quit!

Matt's attempt to catch a few winks was futile now that reveille was only thirty minutes away. Instead of trying to get back to sleep Matt rolled onto his side and surveyed the somber interior of the large hangar. He peered into the dark, looking across the open space at the distorted shapes of his men. They lay scattered about, twisted in random sleeping positions on the cold cement floor. Matt never stopped marveling at the professionalism of these fine sailors.

Each man in Matt's SEAL platoon had arrived at this point in his life by traveling a different path. The person laying closest to him was Boone Kilpatrick. Young Boone had joined the United States Navy after two frustrating years of local community college where he'd attempted to study commercial art. Boone's six-foot frame was well muscled. While appearing thin in clothes, Boone was deceptively strong. He was one of the only men in the platoon without a competitive sports background.

Boone had impressed his boot camp company commander with his natural athletic ability during a weekend sports competition. After sweeping many of the events, Boone was sent to see the resident SEAL recruiter assigned to the Great Lakes, Illinois, recruit training facility. A grizzled old chief talked him into trying out for the teams. He breezed through the SEAL physical screening test. Afterwards, Boone watched a short film about the SEAL teams. He was hooked. With his sandy hair and boyish charm, he always seemed ready to go for it. Matt had great confidence in Boone's instincts. He was the recon team's point man.

Chief Auger lay on the other side of Matt. The chief was an old hand at the special warfare business. Throughout his thirteen years in the teams he'd participated in various minor and major combat actions ranging from advisory work in Central America to Operation Desert Storm. The chief was undoubtedly the strongest man in the platoon. His speed and quickness made him a deadly opponent during close-quarters combat. It was no coincidence that Chief Auger was the command's hand-to-hand combat expert.

His soft-spoken demeanor belied the intensity of his underlying passion and his deep sense of responsibility for the young SEALs he led. The chief had a great bedside manner with the men and with his untested officer. He never belittled or chastised the troops in a public forum. The chief believed you were much more effective as a leader if you praised in public and punished in private. Matt felt especially lucky to have him as his second in command.

Sam Oberman, or Oby, was Matt's over educated enlisted frog. He'd lettered in four different sports through high school, and eventually earned a full wrestling scholarship to attend Boston College. While on Spring break during his senior year, Oby bumped into a group of enlisted SEALs engaged in a rather alcoholic celebration. Earlier that day the men had finally received their well-deserved SEAL insignia, or "Budweiser."

The new SEALs explained to Oby that it still took close to another year after the BUD/S course to complete all the pre-requisites necessary to become a SEAL. Oby stared at the large gold badge with fascination. The metal pin depicted a fierce eagle with wings outstretched. Its claws clutched Neptune's trident and a flintlock pistol. At first glance it did remind Oby of the famous Budweiser logo.

After shooting the breeze with the enlisted SEALs late into the night, Oby knew he was hooked. He graduated later that year with a degree in political science and promptly departed for boot camp in Orlando. Oby graduated from the BUD/S course as class honor man. A distinction bestowed upon the top student as seen through the eyes of his peers. Oby picked up a loose sniper school slot by being in the right place at the right time. He completed the course with flying colors and joined the platoon a week before Matt. Oby was the platoon's sniper.

Next to Oby lay Doc McDermott, the babe magnet in the platoon. The other guys loved to hang around him on liberty waiting to pickup the girls Doc rejected. His smooth charm and movie star good looks always got him out of trouble. Doc made it through BUD/S despite his borderline physical condition. No matter how hard he tried, Doc always found himself at the back of the pack on platoon runs and ocean swims. The guys loved him anyway because despite being the team's worst athlete, he never quit anything he started.

As corpsman for the SEAL platoon, he was a graduate of over two years of advanced special operations medical training. SEAL medical personnel were required to attend the army's advanced Special Forces medic school at Fort Sam Houston, Texas. Doc did extremely well, scoring high enough to be considered for a medical officer's commission. He'd declined, deciding instead to report aboard SDV Team two. Doc wanted to be a shooter, not a cake eater.

Matt could barely see Miguel Cruise, lying against the hangar wall. Miguel was from El Paso, Texas, and was a die-hard Cowboys fan. He was on his second SEAL tour having spent his first five years with SEAL Team Four. While at Team Four, his Latino heritage had been invaluable in conducting counter-drug operations in South and Central America. Cruise saw action in Panama and led a reconnaissance team ashore in support of the aborted invasion of Haiti.

Miguel was discovered during a special language screening process. The teams were looking at all the boot camp populations as part of the SEAL community's effort to increase their Spanish-speaking capability. Cruise immediately embraced the lifestyle and attitude of the U.S. Navy SEAL. He was voted the honor man of his BUD/S training class and was on the ass of anyone who slacked off in the platoon. Cruise was a weapons specialist.

Mitchell Jorgenson and Tim Wells were the last two men in the platoon. Each were new guys, right out of the BUD/S box. Jorgy was a former High school football stud that wasn't quick enough to play college ball. His large size and remarkable stamina earned him the right to carry the seventeen-pound M-60 machine gun and its heavy ammunition.

Jorgy never stopped complaining. He hated point men and their elf-like manner of dancing through the woods while he humped the machinegun. He wasn't fond of officers either. Matt was aware the jury was still out regarding Jorgy's acceptance of him as a platoon commander. Matt saw it as a challenge. If he could impress Jorgy the rest of the team would be easy to inspire.

At the opposite end of the personality spectrum was Tim Wells. He stood five feet, five inches tall. Wells was easily the smallest man in the platoon. He grew up in Hawaii and professed to be a surfer of some ability. His life took a dramatic turn one day when he spotted a mini-sub in Pearl Harbor. Wells went over to the ramp where the SDV support crew was waiting and introduced himself.

He made it a point to return as often as possible over the next year, learning as much as the SEALs would divulge about the unique underwater vehicle. Unfortunately, once in SDV training himself two years later, Wells found he was a terrible mini-sub sailor. Like Matt, he was salvaged and placed in the newly formed direct action/reconnaissance platoon. Wells was responsible for radio communications. He was the only guy who could calm Jorgy down once he was spun up.

Matt turned his head and stared at the ceiling. In the last two months he had feverishly worked to keep up with the operational tempo set by LCDR Sandoval. The entire reconnaissance element was essentially being punished for Matt's late arrival. Having missed the early pre-deployment command and control assessments, Matt was required to participate in the final operational readiness exercise, or ORE, without the benefit of a gradual training program.

His head still throbbed from the effort of memorizing the multitude of valves and gauges associated with the Dry Deck Shelter (DDS). The shelter was a large garage placed piggyback on a U.S. submarine with a SDV or multiple rubber boats in its cargo hold. Each SEAL was required to understand enough about the shelter's operation to help in an emergency. Added to this was the requirement to memorize all the grid coordinates, radio frequencies, call signs and code words to be used on the exercise.

As the reconnaissance platoon commander, Matt rarely navigated a SDV these days. His primary focus now was the combat rubber raiding craft. The SEALS deployed their black CRRCs from the mouth of the submarine mounted DDS to support clandestine infiltration and exfiltration of mission teams. All the task unit SEALs had been required to attend a comprehensive two week DDS course, to learn the system's basic operation and to refresh their advanced deep diving skills. They were then selectively chosen to qualify on several DDS operating stations.

This, along with standard SEAL training in demolitions, weapons, and small unit tactics, made for quite a hectic pre-mission schedule. As always, hard work tended to burn the calendar up, and already Matt wondered what had happened to all the time the platoon had before deploying. Although the guys were looking sharp, using the DDS in the final ORE was putting them way behind the power curve. Matt sighed. Like most SEALS, he was adept at screening out negative thoughts. Hell week taught you that.

Keeping focused and alert while staying awake for five straight days and nights taught you two important things about yourself; first, if you could survive five days of punishment and zero sleep you could probably handle anything. And second, this survival ability was rare among men. Hell week was the fifth week of the difficult twenty-six week course.

By the time Hell week began the class was usually whittled down to forty to fifty sailors and officers. After Hell week only twenty or so would be left standing. The SEAL community's commitment to this Darwinian process was the key to survival during the remaining twenty-one weeks in BUD/S, and to continuing confidence and aggressiveness in the teams. Staff weenies, wives and girlfriends were distractions to be filed away until the mission, or deployment for that matter, was completed successfully. The Team and the men in his platoon came first–period!

NATO Command Headquarters–Naples, Italy

Navy Commander Frank Mason sighed in relief. The briefing had been a rousing success. The NATO commander, Rear Admiral Samuel H. Carden, was more than pleased. He openly congratulated his tired operations staff, taking a moment praise Commander Mason's professional presentation.

"As you know only too well, gentlemen, the detailed mission planning and logistics management required for proper execution of an operation this complex, often spells the difference between success and failure on the battlefield. I want you all to know that I'm flying to Stuttgart, Germany, this evening to brief the European Command on Operation Sparrow Hawk, the invasion of Egypt. I believe my recommendations to the commander will be received favorably, due in no small part to your efforts this last month and a half."

With that said, Admiral Carden and his entourage abruptly departed the small secure briefing room through a side door. Commander Mason tried to keep up with the admiral. He was both elated and nervous. Despite the clear win scored by his planning team today, no one was as tuned into the obvious difficulties associated with Operation Sparrow Hawk as he was. For that reason a small part of him hoped the idea would quietly go away once the big boys took a look at it.

Admiral Carden's stride was vigorous as he left the secure briefing center. Although he was still obliged to personally brief the CINC tomorrow, the time line set by the State Department demanded his quick passing of codeword authorization for Operation Sparrow Hawk to indicate his approval to the president. In this manner the United States national command authority in Washington, could, if required, commit to the initial stages of troop deployment and repositioning of combat support assets within the next one hundred hours.

The admiral pondered the effort involved. In only eight weeks his people had put together an outstanding answer to the Egyptian problem.

Operation Sparrow Hawk would be a lighting raid on a massive scale—seizing key transportation facilities such as airports and harbors to facilitate a massive multinational evacuation of Egypt. Of course, it was looking more and more like NATO was going to delay committing their forces until after the United States was sucked into full unilateral execution.

The plan needed more work. The admiral was especially concerned about the early special operations phase prior to sending the whole task force into Egypt. The SEALS and Green Beret operators would be inserted in the early hours of the operation without air cover or supporting arms. As usual, their missions would be critical to the overall success of Operation Sparrow Hawk. His chief of staff saluted and left the admiral for his operations room.

The admiral entered his stateroom and walked casually toward the oak credenza behind his ornate desk. His eyes were irresistibly drawn toward the black and white photo of his former squadron mates. The A-6 Intruder pilots looked invincible in their faded flight suits, their grinning faces hiding the fear and tension of flying combat missions day in and day out over Hanoi. Only half of the twenty-two men in the picture ever returned home.

Admiral Carden kept the picture close as a reminder of just how bad it could get at the pointy end of the spear. So he would never forget the individual sacrifice asked of each soldier, sailor and airman going into harm's way.

The flag officer turned away from the photo and slumped heavily into his leather office chair. Rubbing his eyes with the palms of his hands, he began again to run over the weak spots in the sparrow hawk plan. Would NATO go through with the operation as planned? And if the European politicians balked, would the United States execute Operation Sparrow Hawk unilaterally? And what if the critical first phase didn't go off as planned? Too many questions, too many unknowns. Admiral Carden looked over once again at those smiling friends of days gone by. Was it ever any different? The men in the picture didn't answer.

Autec Naval Training Area–The Bahamas

The dark seawater rushed into the empty dry deck shelter, pumping in furiously through several small but efficient pipes located in the bottom of the hangar. Matt and the other SEALS could not help reacting to the cool rush of seawater, several of them taking a quick intake of breath. Although the water was extremely warm by Virginia standards, it still took some getting used to. As the water level eased up it became easier for the men to move around in their mission clothing.

The two rolled CRRCs competed with the equipment bags and outboard engines for dominance in the cramped confines of the main hanger. There were three operational DDS chambers. An emergency treatment chamber, a submarine access chamber, and a cargo hangar. For tonights mission the SDV had been removed to allow Matt's platoon to execute a submerged rubber boat launch. The reconnaissance platoon was still bushed after its whirlwind logistical movement to the forward operating base in Puerto Rico.

The operational readiness exercise was designed to not only test the platoon's tactical ability, but also to comprehensively evaluate the SEAL Team's capability to move its operational SEAL platoons and support units where needed with little or no notice.

The dry deck shelter capable submarine had picked up the platoon in Puerto Rico after Matt and his men spent a week rehearsing the mission plan on Pineros Island. They practiced the various phases of their mission based on their planning effort in the isolation area back in Virginia.

The Pineros Island facility was located seven miles off the main island of Puerto Rico. The SEALs unique jungle training site acted as a free fire zone for the practice of live fire direct action missions such as ambushes, demolition raids and sniper supported ground operations. The training area wasn't only used as a rehearsal site. Each year, all the east coast SEAL teams rotated platoons through various maritime training. Pineros was unique in that it allowed the SEALs access to live fire ground targets from the sea.

Matt was pleased with their progress. He believed the rehearsal training had hardened his platoon and kept his guys focused. He knew the proper execution of the pre-mission planning and briefing phase was critical to the success of the operational readiness evaluation. While the confinement and close living arrangements in the Virginia isolation complex tended to agitate the young SEAL warriors, the open-air live fire environment of Pineros Island facilitated the return of their professional passion and an intense desire to succeed. It stirred in all of them a primal hunting instinct. The pre-game show was over, it was time to rock and roll!

Chapter Four

The Dry Deck Shelter was flooded up to the dark painted line on the wall that indicated the safe flood point in the hangar. The navy diver standing in the control bubble spun a tall wheel valve, shutting off the water flow into the hangar. The small space was called the control bubble because the seawater was prevented from flooding the space by pressurization, leaving the operator dry from the waist up.

The hangar supervisor also stood in the bubble keeping dry enough to see the launch and recovery activity in the hangar and to use the command, control and communications suite. The supervisor controlled everything in the DDS from behind a clear Plexiglas window. The first and second-class divers assigned to the DDS were handpicked from throughout the U.S. Navy, and were graduates of rigorous advanced special operations training. The divers and SEALs worked as a cohesive unit to load, unload and operate the DDS system. The divers were physically fit and could pair up comfortably with any SEAL if he needed assistance underwater.

There was a senior diver in charge of the hangar space who coordinated launch/recovery activity using hand and arm signals. He took direction from the supervisor standing behind the window and passed the instructions to the hangar dive team.

The hangar divers received okay signals from each of the SEALs subsequent to pressurizing the shelter to equalize the enclosed shelter with the outside seawater depth. The men used their fingers to pinch their noses. By blowing hard against their nose to open their ears, they allowed the inside chambers of their sinuses to relieve the buildup of sea pressure.

Once equalization between the hangar and sea pressure was complete, a hand signal was passed and the chamber operator hydraulically pumped the huge dry deck shelter door open. As it opened soft starlight to began to filter down from the ocean's surface to the deck of the submarine below. The divers and Matt's eight-man team moved smoothly about the submarine's deck coordinating their various functions like a well-rehearsed underwater ballet.

The Navy divers moved out on deck carrying canvas bags filled with rigging lines. They swam to hard points; stainless steel pad eyes attached to the deck, and snapped the rigging lines in place. Once the lines were ready, a diver took a large deflated salvage buoy out of the hangar and swam out to the middle of the deck. The loose ends of the rigging lines were snapped into the bottom of the large buoy. Then a toggle was pulled, activating the carbon dioxide cylinder attached to the buoy. The buoy shot to the surface of the dark ocean inflating and ascending until all the rigging lines were deployed and standing.

The first object brought out and secured to the deck was a rolled up CRRC. Boone and one of the divers quickly unrolled the boat until it lay flat. They then went back and brought out the second boat. Wells and Jorgy brought out the thirty-five horsepower outboard engines, protected in special rubber waterproof bags. The engines were placed into the boat and secured with metal snap link connectors.

Matt and the remaining SEALs ferried out the additional mission equipment and snapped the bags into both unrolled CRRCs. Fuel bladders were then removed from the submarine's aft line-locker and secured in place next to the outboard engines. The entire process took no more than five minutes during which the submarine maintained perfect trim and depth control. The boats were then snapped into the rigging lines. When the silent dance on deck was finally complete, Matt assembled his mission team on one side of the equipment using a red chemical light stick.

On his signal one man pulled the handle of the carbon dioxide bottle attached to the first CRRC. The team held on as the CRRC gently inflated and lifted off the deck toward the turbulent surface above, guided and tether by the rigging. The second boat was deployed to the surface in the same manner. The operational readiness exercise was underway.

White House Situation Room–Washington, D.C.

President Russell sat quietly listening to the commentary provided by National Security Advisor Allen Cranstan. The chief executive was weary of these sessions. His campaign for president had been based on an America first theme. He had promised the American people a draw down of the military and substantial reinvestment of the peace dividend into his rather aggressive domestic agenda. But as with countless presidents before him, he was now being forced against his will and better judgment to dance to another tune.

It never ceased to amaze him. No matter how bad things were in America, they always seemed to pale in comparison to the crisis of the decaying new world order. President Russell rubbed his tired eyes and forced himself to focus on his friend and national security advisor.

"So in conclusion Mr. President, it's the security council's collective opinion that the problem in Egypt will get worse before it gets better. It's our consensus recommendation that you grant authority to conduct preliminary operations in support of Admiral Carden's contingency plan for the rapid evacuation of American personnel from Egypt. We further request your sanction of Operation Sparrow Hawk with a one hundred hour contingency response window effective one week from today."

The President looked intently at the chairman of the joint chiefs. Air Force General "Bull" Swanson knew what was coming.

"General, I know you and the chiefs have reviewed and approved the Sixth Fleet contingency plan. But what's the down side in doing this before these people in Egypt manifest hostile intent? I mean, there's no indication that I'm aware of, that we should expect a new fundamentalist government to actively seek out and target United States citizens. Aren't we being a little paranoid on this one?"

The ruggedly built general officer choked back his first response. Although by law the president was the commander in chief of the armed forces of the United States, and therefore the chairman's superior, it was the general's personal and professional opinion that this particular president's policies had directly led to the decline of American power, prestige and influence overseas. Thus, by appearing weak to the tyrants and jackals of the world, the president had opened the door for a crisis to occur, maybe in Egypt.

"Mr. President," the chairman began. "Operation Sparrow Hawk is a smart, economical plan using only minimal force to achieve the primary evacuation objectives. The force package required utilizes our special operations forces early on, and relies on army Rangers and marines to establish the evacuation sites and safe corridors in and around Cairo and Alexandria."

The president seemed distracted during the presentation. It was possible he was ignoring the input on purpose. The chairman chose to proceed anyway.

"Mr. President, in my professional opinion there is no downside to the contingency plan submitted by Admiral Carden. Of course, the flow of sufficient pre-mission intelligence will determine how surgical and bloodless the operation will be. This, of course, must be collected well before the one hundred-hour trigger is pulled. With all due respect, Mr.

President, without your authorization to collect such information now, there is the potential for a blood bath on D-Day."

The president clenched his teeth and looked away. His eyes rested on a painting on the wall. He so disliked these military types. So willing to throw bombs at every problem. His eyes strayed to the impressive piece on the wall depicting a scene from the battle of Gettysburg during the Civil War. What a terrible couple of days that must have been for President Lincoln. A horrific and costly battle in a terrible war.

I wonder what old Abe would think about the chairman's plan, he thought. What advice would he give me now? I bet Lincoln would have told me to suck it up! That this was what a president gets paid to do. Every president all the way back to George Washington had their domestic agenda derailed by war or impending conflict. And now it's my turn in the barrel.

The president refocused his attention on the military men and advisors in the Oval Office.

"Very well, General Swanson. The Sixth Fleet contingency plan for Egypt is approved. Let Admiral Carden know he can proceed with logistical preparations immediately. I still fervently hope this whole thing blows over before we have to commit our boys to combat."

President Russell scooted his chair back and hurriedly moved toward the door and his next appointment as the assembled advisors scrambled to jump to their feet. Egypt was an important issue but the floods currently wreaking havoc in California were becoming a major media event. As president he had an obligation to show the proper level of concern, personally. He spoke over his shoulder has he departed the room.

"Have the Secretary of the Interior notified that I'll pick him up in Air Force One enroute to California."

The White House chief of staff nodded. "Yes Mr. President."

The President of the United States put Operation Sparrow Hawk out of his mind and left the room. General Swanson couldn't help smiling.

He stood at attention as the president left, his pack of butt kissers chasing close behind. What the old man did not know, mused the chairman, was that elements of the operation were already in motion. There was no way he would have stood by like some weak functionary. He hadn't waited for this president to wring his hands over what to do while time slipped away.

The forces of change in Egypt would have taken advantage of the delay caused by this administration's hesitation. However, now that he had the official green light, the chairman could get down to business and really start to move some tonnage around.

Offshore–Autec, The Bahamas

Chief Auger directed Jorgy to disconnect the CRRC from the rigging. Matt's boat had already pulled away. Jorgy gave the chief a thumbs up and then waved to the diver hugging the buoy. Chief Auger's CRRC roared across the waves to link up with Matt. The diver unhooked the buoy and swam the rigging down to the deck of the submarine. It would take ten minutes to stow the lines and pull everything and everybody back into the DDS.

The two black rubber boats streaked across the surface of the water. The sea parted easily, not minding their hurried passage. Matt's team was ready to get ashore and get down to business. Officially it was day eight of the ORE. But the real game started now. It felt great to finally get away from the submarine. The SEALs were tired of the endless planning and briefing.

Studying DDS launch procedures, target parameters, timetables and all the other issues related to the ORE mission. They were also sick of being watched daily, by staff pukes grading the pre-mission phases. LCDR. Sandoval, in particular, had been a royal pain in the butt for everyone involved. The flabby desk commando had contested every detail of the operation. It was a miracle, Matt thought, that the man hadn't demanded a ride in the CRRC! But of course that would've meant getting wet and cold and maybe even speaking with real enlisted men.

LCDR Sandoval was so unlike any SEAL officer Matt had ever met or worked with, that sometimes he wondered if the man had somehow faked his way into the teams. Matt looked over at the second CRRC trailing slightly behind and to the left of his lead boat. Boone was using a night observation device, or NOD, to pick out coastal navigation lights. Behind him Cruise was plotting the fixes provided by Boone onto a Plexiglas navigation board. Even though they were in the trail boat, Chief Auger was making sure they backed up Matt's primary navigation team, just in case they made a mistake.

It had been close to two and a half hours since the successful dry deck shelter launch. Matt looked down at a nautical chart segment made of special waterproof paper. His calculations put them about two miles offshore. Matt turned to Wells.

"What's up Wells? Any chance we'll get out of this damn boat before the sun comes up?"

The platoon's primary navigator was a professional. Although only a third class petty officer, he excelled at nearly every aspect of SEAL operations.

"Keep your pants on, sir!" Wells whispered. "All we have left to do now is lock on a satellite fix in about two minutes, then zig right a bit, follow the coast line for five hundred yards or so, and presto! We'll get a final satellite fix once there and confirm our insert point."

Smiling in the dark, he added, "What's the matter sir, don't you trust me?"

Matt now regretted raising the question in the first place. One of the strangest things about the teams was the quality of individual you found working alongside you. Men who excelled at anything they set their minds to. All of them content to be on-loan to Uncle Sam's navy. Each man doing it for the right to be called, a Navy SEAL.

As predicted, Wells directed Oby to come right onto a course running parallel to the beach. Matt couldn't see the shoreline but he knew Wells' partner in crime, Jorgy, was using a night observation device to track their progress. As the boat maneuvered around to its new base course, Jorgy whispered, "Mark!"

This call indicated to Wells that the boat's nose was now on the correct course parallel to the shore. Wells noted the magnetic heading and told Oby to hold that course. The second boat slid around to the right after executing the turn and continued to maintain its position. Matt knew the chief was continuing to make Boone and the others work on the backup navigation team to make sure the LT didn't screw up. Matt didn't take his chief 's initiative personally. If Chief Auger hadn't been doing this drill on his own, Matt would have directed him to do it anyway. Chief Auger's value as a sounding board continued to help Matt anticipate potential problems and prepare for them. As mentors go, Chief Auger was one of the best.

The overhead photography didn't show the coral reef at low tide, so there was no way the SEALs could know for sure whether or not they could take the boats straight into the beach landing site. Wells signaled to Oby to slow down by gently pressing his open palm toward the surface of the water. As both CRRCs backed down, Matt took the night observation scope from Jorgy to check things out for himself.

The view afforded him by the sophisticated night vision device elicited a low groan from Matt. The tide was at just the right height to allow the offshore waves to mark the reef line. The bitch of it was, if they waited there too long, there was an outside chance the tide would go further out, thus uncovering the actual reef itself. This would make it fairly easy to pick out an opening wide enough to get the rubber boats through to the beach safely. The real question was, did they have enough time to sit around and find out?

Wells raised a clenched fist indicating he wanted the boats to stop. Matt lowered the scope and patiently awaited the navigator's verdict. Wells glanced back to respond to the lieutenant's unspoken question.

"I just took a global positioning fix, boss. Best I can figure we're close enough for government work!"

Matt checked his watch. One thirty in the morning. That left three and a half hours until nautical twilight began. At sea, dawn came early, offering visibility an hour or so before the sun actually broke the horizon. The SEALs needed to be underway and en route to the submarine rendezvous before this early illumination.

Chief Auger maneuvered his CRRC along the port side of the lead boat to see what the hell was going on. It was apparent from his backup teams analysis that they were at the right point.

"Why aren't we going in, LT?"

Matt reached out to grab the carrying handle of the chief's boat, stabilizing the two boats immediately. Wells hissed a warning to Chief Auger.

"Hey, chief! Put your engine in neutral, you're shoving us toward the coral!"

The chief glanced shoreward and quickly gestured to Cruise to kill the outboard on the second boat. The chief then turned his attention back to the reason he'd pulled alongside in the first place.

"So what gives, boss? Are we going in or what?"

Before Matt could answer, Wells closed the waterproof box containing the global positioning unit with a loud snap!

"Bingo, big cheese, we are definitely at beach-center. Chalk up one more for the kid!"

The chief and Matt both smiled at hearing the good news from Wells. No matter how much the platoon planned and worked to get this stuff right, there were always ways to screw it up. Every SEAL had a sea bag full of horror stories from previous training missions. The tradition was to start your tale with the phrase, "so there I was." Invariably the stories included other factors which increased the drama of the experience such as storms, freezing temperatures, unbelievable forced marches, and all night ocean swims in shark infested waters. As one might expect, these sea stories became more tragic and fantastic with each telling.

"That's good news, Wells, and you did a fine job getting us here."

Matt's comment stated the obvious. Nobody in the teams took this shit for granted. The lieutenant was speaking for the entire platoon.

"All right, chief." Matt turned once again to look directly at the senior enlisted man. "The way I see it, we don't have time to wait around for the tide to help us out and we can't take a chance at losing these boats by running them through the coral reef. So my idea is to drop anchor near the far right flank of this beach and infiltrate by swimming in."

"How far a swim ya figure that's going to be, LT?" Chief Auger asked.

"It doesn't really matter how far, chief," Matt replied. "It's our final exam and we don't have a choice in the matter. We're going to get the job done. Comprende?"

The chief held up both hands and shook his head.

"You're the boss man, LT. Whatever you say. But let's get going, we're burning moonlight just sitting here."

The loud booming waves breaking on the dark and ominous reef line finally registered in Matt's consciousness. He glanced over to observe the chief's efforts to secure the boats to each other. The boat pool would stay anchored just thirty yards seaward of the first breaker line. On the lieutenant's order, six of the platoon's fearsome gun-slingers slid quietly out of their respective combat rubber raiding craft and into the dark ocean. The chief waved and whispered good luck as he watched them disappear in the distance.

The mild chill of the water reminded everyone of how depleted their energy reserves were already. The time spent immersed in the DDS had taken a toll on the fluid levels in their bodies. In the warm waters off the Bahamas, a swimmer's body would continuously sweat. Within an hour or so a man could lose enough water through perspiring to flirt with mild hypothermia. Add an open-air boat trip, followed by a pleasant night swim to the beach and you were looking at a condition that could negatively impact on mission success.

Boone and Doc led the swimmers into the reef, all of them straining to see if there really was an opening large enough for the swimmers. It was impossible at this stage to see anything of the shore. What had seemed simple navigation from the raised platform of their boats was now made difficult by the rising and falling ocean swells. Boone tried to use the angle of the wave sets to determine a good heading to the beach-landing site. He backed this up from time to time with a quick check of his wrist compass. Just finding the shore was easy, any piece of crap tossed overboard ended up there eventually.

The problem the SEALs had in this case was to prevent being swept far left or right of the intended BLS. Jagged rocks protected the coastline everywhere but on their beach-landing site. Matt felt anxious as the group crashed through the first line of breakers. His concern was erased however when the team all managed to pop up on the other side intact. The men had instinctively bunched up prior to negotiating the first challenge. Now they were spread out.

Each of them wore the old reliable UDT life jacket developed by early frogmen to be simple and reliable. This critical piece of equipment had remained in the team's inventory for longer than anyone could remember. While it was a great way to compensate for the weight of bullets and guns if you fell overboard, it was a pain in the butt if used as flotation support during a swim. If used in this manner it turned a SEAL into an uncontrollable one-man raft, subject to the movement of every wave and current that came along.

SEALs were trained from day one in BUD/S to respect the sea. Full combat equipment swims carrying ammunition, food, water, demolition packs and radio gear, were routine events in every phase of SEAL training. Throughout this educational process the men learned how to sew high-density foam into their battle harness and associated pouches to compensate for the dead weight of combat equipment. Inflatable bladders taken from demolition haversacks completed the flotation scheme.

M-60 machine gunners often had to carry two UDT life jackets to make it work. One for the swimmer and one to float the weapon. Boone signaled for Matt to swim closer. Matt reduced the distance with a few powerful short strokes of his fins.

"What's up?" Matt whispered.

"No dice, boss," Boone sputtered. "There's just no way through but straight over the top of this coral."

A small wave smacked Matt in the face before he could respond. Boone twisted his head just in time to avoid getting a mouth full of sea-water from the same wave.

"Well boss, it looks like we're going kamikaze body surfing with guns!"

Matt's face reflected his concern. All the frogmen were again clustering in a dog pile around him, kicking and kneeing each other in the process. Matt's consideration of Boone's assessment was accelerated by a sharp knee in the lower back.

"Okay Boone, take us through before we kill each other out here!"

Matt turned and filled the other swimmers in on his decision to go over the coral.

"Boys, here's the deal. There's no way through the reef as far as we can tell from here so we're swimming in over this mess. We just don't have time to screw around any more."

As he spoke the men nodded in agreement. They were all starting to shiver. The coral or hypothermia, it wasn't much of a choice. At least they could warm up once ashore.

CHAPTER FIVE

The first cut was small. Matt's knee vaguely registered pain. That was until the salt water seeped into the tiny wound. Within seconds he banged into another coral head and felt the sharp edge cutting into his thigh. Matt then heard muffled profanity off to his left, a sure sign he wasn't the only guy getting beat up.

Within twenty minutes of hard swimming the main reef line lay well behind them. Looking seaward over his shoulder, Matt confirmed the total invisibility of his boat. The frogmen swam for five more minutes. Soon Matt's fingertips dug into the sandy bottom. A few powerful kicks later all the SEALs were well into shallow water. Pointing the waterproof night vision scope toward the shoreline, Matt could make out a continuous line of low brush and small bent trees.

The trees grew at sharp angles to the ground here on the windward side of the island. Matt's best guess was they were approximately thirty yards away from the pre-selected beach-landing site. Matt signaled Boone and the other SEALs to advance online to the beach. Boone and Jorgy moved ahead of the rest as planned. They both drained their weapons as they closed the distance to the beach.

Boone moved in front of Jorgy and his M-60 machine gun, taking point in their two-man patrol. Both half-crawled, half-crouched, as they left the water and stepped onto dry land. The swimmer scout pair patrolled carefully in a diamond shaped pattern. This tactical maneuver would take them fifteen yards into the backshore in a round about way. At each point of the pattern Boone and Jorgy paused to look and listen to the night sounds.

After a moment or two they moved to the next point and repeated the process. Matt and the rest of the SEALs stayed in waist deep water, spread out in a firing line. They aimed their weapons toward the outside edges of the diamond. If enemy fire came from the backshore area, the platoon members in the water could engage and support Jorgy and Boone without hitting them.

Matt's job was to alternate firing illumination rounds and forty millimeter grenades far inland and walking them back towards the beach landing site. This technique panicked an attacking force as they were squeezed between the exploding rounds and the SEALs on the beach. The illumination flares would effectively back light the attackers while keeping the SEALs in darkness. Matt and the rest of the SEALs would continue to fire their weapons until the swimmer scout pair returned to the waters edge and rejoined the rest of the SEALs.

Boone signaled the letter "sierra" in Morse code with his green penlight to indicate to Matt that they could come ashore safely. He then moved back to the sandy ridgeline with Jorgy to set up point security at the top of the diamond pattern. The dark shapes contrasted sharply with the moon lit sand as the rest of the team darted one at a time across the tiny sliver of open beach to join them. As each man arrived, Boone pointed out where to set up. The end result was a defense perimeter and a full head count.

Matt moved to the center of the circle and the SEALs began the standard ten-minute drill. Look, listen and wait. Matt sneaked a quick look at his luminescent dive watch to see how they were doing with time. His brow knitted in consternation as he calculated the rest of their transit quietly in his mind. In every special operations mission the planning team tossed in a little extra time to allow for screw-ups.

This "fudge factor" allowed the team leader to expand or contract the mission time line once he was on the ground.

Unfortunately for Matt and the platoon, the unexpected night swim to the beach had used up all the slack. The ten minutes passed without incident. Matt motioned for Boone to move out. The team eased out of the defensive perimeter, uncoiling like a dark green serpent. Each man in turn stood up and assumed his position in the patrol. The SEALs carefully placed every step, their quiet passage barely registering a complaint from the jungle life all around them.

City Of The Dead–Cairo, Egypt

Banadar was very relaxed under the ancient olive tree. Its twisted branches offered welcome shelter against the intense Egyptian sun. Here in this magical place the sunlight played subtle tricks, casting dancing shadows on the ground in front of him. The effect was as soothing as it was mesmerizing. Banadar sat cross-legged, quietly contemplating his most recent move, calculating what effect his planned acts of violence were having on his intended audience.

Since the beginning of the struggle, his interest had been to raise awareness in the Egyptian people of their power and their destiny. They needed to see and understand what the infidels were doing to their country. The western world had made a whore out of Egypt. And Egypt's leaders were no better than high paid pimps. Selling the people's legacy to the highest bidder. Banadar also had a personal reason to destroy the infidels. Banadar's own uncle had died while under torture after the first bold, but ill-fated strike of the jihad, the holy war against those who would rule from London, Paris, and America.

Banadar needed time to think. Time to carefully consider the next phase of his plan. He wanted violence, yes, but he couldn't afford wasteful losses. There would be time enough for martyrs. Now he needed patience, the patience to wait for the next opportunity to deal a serious blow. Banadar's silent army was frustrated and skittish. The attack against the American communications facility had been a great boost to morale. It also had the added impact of focusing Washington's diplomatic pressure and attention on the weak and impotent Egyptian government.

What he'd failed to do on his own, the foolish government now accomplished for him. The Egyptian state radio and television networks had declared martial law throughout the country soon after the first call from the American state department. They were helping create in the public mind an image that far exaggerated Banadar's actual power and strength. This media blitz was actually giving him and his cause a sort of celebrity status. And now the flow of recruits, which had been but a trickle, was nearly unmanageable.

What the pig-headed puppets had failed to realize was the depth of resentment and loathing residing in the hearts and minds of the Egyptian people. He now had the propaganda arm he had longed for, courtesy of his enemies. The press was doing one more thing that assisted Banadar. They were crafting a near mythical image of him as a great spiritual leader, a leader whose single-minded purpose was to rule the nation by the code of Mohammed.

They portrayed him as a ruthless warrior who would stop at nothing to tear down the existing fabric of Egyptian society, and in this they were right. In their minds and the minds of their audience Banadar was an enigma. He liked that very much. An enigma to his enemies and a holy warrior to his people. Well then, so be it! So much the better for him, and for the cause. He stood up, stretching his wiry frame. Banadar yawned and focused his thoughts on today's scheduled events.

Soon he would travel to a dusty gathering place secluded from curious or idle strangers. The Egyptian air force and navy were ready to negotiate for a place in his new fundamentalist regime. Banadar was willing to give them anything they wanted to gain their support of the final phase of the Jihad. However, once the deed was done, he could swiftly erase the dogs from Egypt and place his own loyal lieutenants in command. For now, let them think they are in control.

"Beloved one, the truck is ready behind that wall."

The husky man turned after speaking and gestured toward the eight-foot rock wall that surrounded the small grove of olive trees.

"Is everything else in order?"

Banadar's voice was as always just barely audible, which seemed to make other men listen more and talk less in his presence. The trusted bodyguard looked deep into the startling black eyes and swallowed hard before answering.

"Yes my Lord. All is in order. The generals will be there ahead of us, and there will be plenty of time to allow us to sweep the area for traps."

"Have you contacted our people at the meeting place?" asked Banadar.

"Well uh, yes, of course we did, my Lord. If you'd like, we can call them now."

Banadar looked up at the big man, focusing on his eyes. The bodyguard's face was pinched in a nervous squint. He dully returned his master's stare.

"Fine. Then call them now and tell them to move the generals to Askari. Tell them to take the King Khaled highway and wait at the entrance to the quarry for further instructions."

With that said, Banadar moved purposefully toward the waiting truck.

Autec–The Bahamas

Boone was in his element. The fact that SEALs were experts at maritime infiltration and exfiltration was well established. What wasn't as well known was their natural ability to blend into almost any terrain or environment. SEALs loved to play sneak and peek. They were good at it, and regardless of the opinion of their marine and army brothers in arms, the SEALs were undeniably the best in the world.

The center of the island sloped up to form a spine like ridge running north and south. Boone grunted as he stumbled up the dark incline. Matt followed close behind trying to maintain close physical contact in the inky darkness. The men were all warmed up now, the heat of their drying cammies steaming off them in lazy tendrils.

Twice during the two-kilometer climb they were forced to detour around campfires lying directly in their path. Even though the island's inhabitants were out of play, they didn't want to be spotted. The SEALs pride was at stake. The patrol stopped just short of the top, turning right to move parallel to the ridgeline. It took another half hour to reach the height dominating the east end of the island. Once there, Matt halted the patrol and took out the night vision scope.

Scanning intently, Matt noticed a flickering light not far from the original beach-landing site. Down near the far right flank of the beach below. Taking the scope from his eye he turned and offered it to Boone to see if his point man could also pick it out.

"See if you spot anything strange down there, Boone?"

Matt gestured, pointing toward the beach in the distance. Boone nodded and took a knee. With this added stabilization he was able to not only detect the same phenomenon that Matt had, but he also was able to see actual movement in the tree line along the beach.

"Well, what do you think?" Matt whispered." Anything to worry about here?"

"Only if you consider a bunch of assholes hiding at our original beach landing-site something to worry about!" Boone exclaimed.

Matt snatched the scope away from Boone and knelt down to take a better look.

"Sure as shit, said Matt. "Now how in the Hell did those bozos figure out exactly which part of which beach to set up on?"

Snickering from behind caused Matt to turn.

"Well boss, I wouldn't put it past those staff pukes to hand out color copies of the mission brief you gave to LCDR Sandoval just to screw us over!"

Wells was grinning as he spoke up. It was the same old game. The staff guys hated the young operators because they were the shooters and the staff personnel's days of operating were ancient history. So they pulled bullshit stunts like this one.

"I remember one time the Echo platoon guys got in a pissing contest with some of the training department guys. They were in Blackstone, Virginia, in a bar and the shit really hit the fan. Echo won the fight, of course. When their ORE came up six months later, the training guys set the platoon up to fail. Echo had to do the ORE all over again."

"Yeah!" chimed in Doc. "I remember that too. The skipper heard a rumor of what went down and reamed the training department. Echo platoon still had to repeat the damn ORE though. You know LT, the training guys don't like us much either. And Sandoval has a serious case of the ass for you, and that's a fact. No sir, I wouldn't put it past these guys to jerk us around tonight!"

Matt nodded in silent agreement. LCDR Sandoval had been gunning for him ever since his dismal performance in the advanced SDV operator course. The senior officer just flat out refused to see the potential of the new reconnaissance platoon concept. He actually thought Matt was perfect for the leadership job during the test and evaluation phase at SDV Team Two. By allowing Matt to carry the ball, LCDR Sandoval was sure the concept would fail. Then the team could get back to the bread and butter mission he so dearly loved.

As far as Sandoval was concerned, if you were not a top-notch minisub operator you needed to just go somewhere else. The fact that over time Matt and his platoon were in fact responsible for the huge success of the new unit structure pissed Sandoval off even more. If tonight the odds had been stacked against them, Matt and his platoon would just have to level the playing field somehow! Matt motioned for the men to circle up.

"Listen up guys, this is where we give the goons in staff a royal headache. As you all know, back on the sub we told the big wigs we were going to conduct a demolition raid. But you also know I made Oby lug along a fifty cal sniper rifle. An old SEAL instructor back in BUD/S training told my class that back in Nam they always had to worry about their mission plans leaking out in the base area. So they had a saying. A plan for show, and a plan for go! Sandoval and the headquarters pukes watched our show back at the submarine. So listen close, here's my plan for go!"

After Matt's quick patrol brief the SEALs shifted back into a file formation. Matt allowed Oby to come up and join Boone at point. Oby needed to select his final firing point, or FFP. He and Boone scouted the steep ridgeline looking for the lights indicating their target's location.

Oby signaled Boone that he had a good site picked out. Boone moved up quietly to join Oby and act as spotter and loader for the sniper rifle. The fifty had a removable bolt, which was loaded by hand after each shot. Oby and Boone trained back in the States to keep the time lag between shots as short as possible. Matt took the rest of the SEALs and set up a wide semi-circle behind the sniper pair. For the remainder of the actions on target Matt and the others would provide security and leave the killing to Oby.

The four "enemy" soldiers were clustered together near the missile site. They were a mixed bunch, made up of three new SEALs and one navy career counselor trying to get out of the office for a change.

"Boy, these missiles sure look real!" exclaimed a tall blond haired guard. He was a new guy to the team.

"Yeah, they even filled the nose cones with gasoline so they will look cooler when the demolition charges blow!" answered one of the other new guys on target.

The four men began to speculate on where the SEAL platoon would attack. The opinions were split down the middle. Either they would strike from the access road or from the heavy "wait a minute" bushes and the west end of the target area. In either case, LCDR Sandoval and a few trainers had been on site just prior to nightfall directing the new guys to place booby traps three hundred and sixty degrees around the missiles. The area was so saturated the guards couldn't even relieve themselves without tripping a flare or grenade simulator.

The guards returned to an earlier debate on the classic question of which training class went through a tougher hell week? They were completely unaware each had for a brief moment occupied the sight on Oby's Macmillan fifty-caliber rifle. With a final nod from Boone and a quick glance at his dive watch, the SEAL sniper moved his point of aim to the first nose cone and began to squeeze.

The roar of the explosion knocked the aggressors forcefully to the ground. Before they could get up, a second explosion rocked the night. The five-inch long, fifty-caliber explosive tipped RDX round had been originally designed to destroy aircraft parked on enemy airfields. Military aircraft were normally staged ready to fly, fully topped off with fuel. This also helped to reduce the build up of condensation in the fuel lines.

Though the target tonight wasn't as difficult to attack as a real enemy airfield, the effect on the gas-filled missiles was just as spectacular as nailing the real thing. The six man aggressor team, hiding near the originally briefed beach landing site, stopped talking and stared back toward the center of the island as the shock wave rushed by them.

The second blast was even greater, taking away their night vision. From their perspective the platoon was adhering to the original mission timetable. And it was now obvious that the attacking SEAL platoon had given them the slip by coming ashore somewhere else.

"Come on guys, let's go down the beach path and catch them heading to their extract point!" shouted the chief in charge of the aggressor force. He grabbed his rifle and gestured for the others to follow him inland.

"What about the boat, chief?" his partner asked. "Shouldn't we leave someone back to guard the boat?"

The chief looked at the long black boat. The aggressors had inserted administratively by the F-470 rubber boat the day before. It now sat nearby, high enough to avoid the tide.

"No, I'm taking all of you with me. We'll be back as soon as we hit these guys. Leave it and move out now!"

With that discussion ended, the aggressor force trotted along the island path as fast as the limited light and jungle growth would allow them. The path curled towards the ridge inland for about ten minutes then swung back to the beach near the platoon's originally briefed extraction point. The training department instructors were going to pay a little surprise visit on the upstart SEAL platoon. Huffing and puffing in the lead, the aggressor chief didn't see the trip wire until it was too late.

The jungle night erupted in a flash of light and sound as Matt's well-hidden SEALs opened fire. Grenade simulators exploded all around the aggressors who by now had wisely hit the deck. The platoon, led by Matt, swept through the kill zone putting rounds into each body they found. Although they were only using blank ammo, Jorgy's M-60 machine-gun was on full rock and roll and it inspired respect.

Completing their sweep through the kill zone, the SEALs consolidated and sprinted down the path toward the beach. The aggressors scattered all over the path behind them played the game and stayed dead. Something one couldn't always count on during these bullshit exercises.

CHAPTER SIX

Matt slowed the team down. It wouldn't be cool to deal with one ambush correctly only to run right into another one. Doc was running point. He slowed the pace of movement when Matt tapped him on the shoulder. The rest of the SEALs matched the new patrol speed–feeding off the body language of those in front of them.

After traveling for twenty minutes, Matt squeezed Doc's arm. The corpsman froze. Matt pointed to the side of the dark trail indicating the team should move off the trail. Doc stepped into the thick under-growth. Each of the team members did likewise. Once inside the foliage, the SEALs turned to face the path. The SEALs would rest and be able to hit anyone following them form the target site.

Close to the beach, Boone and Wells arrived next to the aggressor's campsite. They settled in and waited quietly in the bushes a few yards from the training department's rubber boat. Boone carefully exposed the face of his dive watch and pushed the light button. He did the math in his head, trying to determine how long it should take for the rest of the guys to show up on the beach.

Wells pointed silently to the encrypted radio at his side. Boone shook his head. There wasn't a reason to break radio silence, at least not yet. Boone and Wells settled in for a long stay. The wind was dieing down. Soon the bloodsucking mosquitoes would be out in force.

Matt checked his watch. They'd been sitting next to the trail for thirty minutes. If the training department planned on chasing them they would've shown themselves by now. Matt poked Doc in the ribs. Doc's head swiveled slowly to lock on Matt. Matt stood up, quietly shifting his weight to reduce the sound of breaking brush. Doc and the rest of the SEALs followed suit. Matt stepped out onto the trail, sweeping his weapon in a wide arch his eyes scanning in sync with his barrel. The others were assembled and awaiting their cue. Matt pointed down the trail and toward the beach. Doc nodded and moved out.

Wells barely heard the cammy pants brushing against each other over the load humming of the pesky insects. He poked Boone in back and at the same time swatted at a cluster of mad bugs trying to reach his brain through his nose.

"Here they come!" Wells whispered.

Boone responded by raising his weapon and pointing it at the point where the trail reached the beach. A minute later Boone watched as Doc slid out of the dark jungle. He saw Doc hold up a clenched fist to stop the patrol. Doc was staring at the black rubber boat sitting on the beach only a few feet away. He was unable to see Boone and Wells, but knew they had to be close. This was the agreed upon rendezvous point for the platoon.

Doc looked back for a moment before stepping further out onto the beach. Matt and the rest of the SEALs followed Doc out of the jungle and stepped to their fields of fire. They knelt down creating a defense position half on and half off the beach. It was time for the bona fide exchange.

Bona fide exchanges occurred when two units were about to make contact in a hostile environment and when the use of radios was excessively dangerous. Normally the coded phrases were easy for tired men to remember. Unlike Hollywood's elaborate concept of secrecy, SEALs stuck to what worked, and what worked was something simple. Matt was using a combination of any two numbers adding up to a total of seven.

"Three!"

Doc initiated by calling out the number, three. He tried to project his voice in a loud whisper. The answer came immediately from the group on the beach.

"Four!"

Since the response added up to the prearranged authentication of seven, Boone and Wells were comfortable. They rose silently from their hiding place and smiled at the other platoon members. The two snipers walked the short distance to the perimeter. The platoon's reunion was brief. Matt directed Jorgy and wells to watch the path leading back into the jungle just in case the training guys got a little froggy. He split the remaining SEALs in half, placing them on the left and right side of the rubber boat.

"I'm sure not looking forward to swimming back out through that crap again," Boone sighed, looking out to sea.

"Who said we had to swim?" said Matt.

He smiled at the surprised point man. Matt motioned for Doc and Boone to help him. The three of them grabbed the CRRC by the side carrying handles and picked up the boat.

"Just like the good old days in Coronado, eh boss?" Doc grimaced. He was recalling the dreaded IBS boat drills experienced during the first phase of the BUD/S program. Most BUD/S candidates were woefully unprepared for the harsh California surf. Winter classes traditionally were devastated by the crunching waves. The entire BUD/S class was divided into boat crews of seven men each. An officer or senior enlisted man was placed in charge of each IBS, or inflatable boat–small. The students were required to carry the 150-pound rubber boat for the first seven weeks of SEAL training.

The IBS surf passage drills were scary, and responsible for most of the class medical attrition. However, most BUD/S students pointed to their experience carrying the boats on their heads, as the worst possible torture. During Hell Week, students spent 120 continuous hours with their boats. The beach sand stuck on the bottom of an IBS, ground the skin on the student's skull, taking much of it right off. SEALs had few fond memories regarding rubber boats.

Matt chuckled. "You got that right. Now quit whining! I want to get this clump into the water!"

Once they had the CRRC floating the Matt signaled for the rest of the team to collapse the security perimeter toward the boat. Each SEAL jumped in assuming firing positions in the boat. At no time were the threat areas ashore left uncovered.

Doc squeezed the fuel ball, shooting a jet of gasoline into the outboard engine. He grabbed the pull toggle and with one rapid jerk the engine roared to life. Jorgy pushed the CRRC out further and was the last to jump into the boat. The SEALs were finally off the beach and heading out toward sea.

Chief Auger sat upright and grabbed the headset as soon as the radio crackled to life. He quickly placed it on his head, his face shrouded in concern.

"I hope everything's all right!" The chief keyed the transmission button. "Hammer, this is Donald Duck, say again your last, over." He listened for a moment as Matt brought him up to speed on the mission and the manner of their extraction. "Roger, hammer, understood–Donald Duck out!" The chief couldn't hide his smile from the others in the boat pool.

"What's going on, chief?" Cruise asked. "They in trouble or what?"

Chief Auger looked around at the boat crew, studying their expressions. "Trouble shit, our boys kicked ass and took names! And to top it off, the LT took the aggressor's boat! They'll be here in a less than thirty minutes."

Matt directed Doc to steer a bit to the left. He could see the other boat at the rendezvous point using his night vision system. Wells leaned out over the bow watching for the reef. The rising tide gave them more room to pass over the tricky barrier. The rest of the SEALs could now see Chief Auger's CRRC without the use of vision aides. Doc turned the boat a little more to the left and throttled down. They had arrived.

The platoon was reunited. They left the captured rubber boat anchored to the coral reef, tying it directly to the horns of the coral to hold it securely in place. "Okay chief, let's get back to the sub before the sun comes up!"

The chief gave Matt the thumbs up signal. "You got it, boss!"

He turned his fully loaded raiding craft to sea. The chief was taking the lead this time. He checked his compass once more and set out, heading for the submarine rendezvous point. Most of the guys were already sacked out in the two boats. It'd been a long night's work.

On the transit to the submarine Matt went over the entire mission, phase by phase. He knew his platoon had executed well. He also knew Sandoval and the other staff types were going to be pissed to no end about his platoon's success. Matt didn't care. In the end only Captain Richard's opinion counted in an ORE. The training department and Sandoval in particular, were going to say the platoon cheated by not following the mission plan. Matt knew in his heart that the CO would see things differently.

They couldn't take this victory from him or his men. Not only were they ready to deploy, in his mind they were ready for anything! Matt thought about Sandoval's many attempts to make Matt look bad. In the end the LCDR had failed to prove Matt was an incompetent SEAL officer. His efforts to challenge him were childish and weak compared to what Matt had endured as a boy. Sandoval, you're a rank amateur compared to my old man! He snuggled into a ball. Sleep came quickly for the SEAL officer.

The Pentagon–Washington, D.C.

The on-duty Pentagon logistics officer absentmindedly sipped the luke warm cup of coffee. The major placed the weathered cup, bearing the Joint Chief of Staff's symbol, back in its normal resting place on the stained desk. The collection of old coffee stains served as mute testimony to the monastic life led by thousands of military functionaries.

These duty-bound gatherers of information performed their thankless routine all around the world, far beyond the view of an unaware and uninterested public. He was doing his time deep in the heart of the nation's five sided military headquarters.

The Joint Chiefs of Staff deployment order 102.1B was a marvel of simplicity and directness. The inch thick stack of commands would communicate the orders of America's high military leaders to every corner of the globe. If the plan required assistance from any service, any unit, any supply depot, the order would make sure they knew about it. This particular order was special to the major. He and only a handpicked few had worked on it for several weeks. While the timeline had been tight, the major felt it was some of his very best work.

In keeping with tradition, JCS Order 102.1B had a proper code name, Operation Sparrow Hawk. The name was the major's idea. His teenage son was interested in birds. Especially predators. The sparrow hawk was a small, yet ruthless, and effective, hunting bird. His son had been working on a school paper when the major was developing the JCS mission order. The lightning strike envisioned in the mission order reminded the major of the aggressive little predator.

Operation Sparrow Hawk called for keeping a low profile in the expected theater of operations during the preparatory phase. The U.S. would work vigorously behind the veil of normalcy to stage all the military forces required to conduct a quick action in Egypt. Elements were even now in place in the Mediterranean that would form the backbone of the Americans' first strike capability.

Other U.S. follow-on forces, from England, Spain and Italy would be used along with selected airflow support out of Germany. While talks were still ongoing, it did not appear now that the NATO nations were going to offer anything by way of help except permission to deploy U.S. military forces from existing NATO bases.

The designated army special forces, and navy special warfare units for the operation were going to rotate into the Eastern Mediterranean under the cover of a few, pre-scheduled NATO interoperability exercises. The American commando units would maintain their normal schedules of forward deployment activity with no actual knowledge of the CON-PLAN, or contingency plan, they were now designated to support.

Other more unique elements such as army's psychological operations teams and civil affairs units, would have to be ordered up from the Reserves and National Guard units. These groups would be sent to staging bases in Italy, also under the guise of NATO peacetime exercise play.

While declining to participate in the initial police action in Egypt, NATO was putting together a second, much larger version of Sparrow Hawk. Their plan would relieve the American forces in place and establish a prolonged presence on the ground. The Europeans would stay in country after the Americans left in order to stabilize the region and peacefully return the legally elected government to power.

The major saved the file, and then ejected the floppy disk he'd been working on. He kicked the main power switch off with the tip of his shoe as he pushed himself out of the clumsy swivel chair. Today was the kickoff date for the operation. Whatever happened in the actual operation, good or bad, the major was sure he would come out smelling like a rose due to the exactness of his work on Sparrow Hawk.

A fine ballet of moving parts that most of the medal hunting grunts actually participating on the ground could not possibly appreciate or understand.

CHAPTER SEVEN

U.S. Naval Air Station–Siganella, Sicily

The hot blast of the navy jet's exhaust seemed to linger a few feet above the blacktop as the platoon, cramped and sluggish from the long flight, struggled to climb out of the aircraft. Looking out of the tiny cargo window Boone could see the rugged terrain of Sicily shimmering in the afternoon sun.

It had been only a month since the successful ORE. Matt's reconnaissance platoon should have been enjoying a well-deserved pre-deployment leave, not flying off to the Med on some training exercise. Captain Richards had been apologetic when he'd handpicked Matt's men to respond to the surprise tasking. He explained it would be a short duration exercise and that the SEAL platoon would be back in the States before they knew it. Matt and his men accepted the captain's words without complaint. This was a part of the deal and they knew it.

It was normal practice for Matt to get off the plane last so he could thank the aircrew and smooth out any problems caused by his guys during the flight. SEALs travel one of two ways; either they sleep like the dead or they pace about like caged tigers. This last option usually pissed off the air force types. They were used to passengers staying put, belted and docile.

On this flight, however, Matt was happy to see there hadn't been any incidents. As he stepped off the large C-141 tail ramp, he looked around to inventory the scenery. His men were already putting it into words.

"This place sucks!"

Boone's sharp announcement received near unanimous agreement from everyone but the chief. "All right, girls, let's get the flatbed truck over here and start unloading this bird!"

The SEALs knew the drill. Do what the chief wanted and liberty would come that much sooner. Screw around, and you pay the price. Chief Auger took care of you if you put out and pitched in. His favorite phase was, there are always good deals for good SEALs. So without a gripe, the young sailors dropped their kit bags, daypacks, radios, and briefcases to begin off loading the huge cargo plane.

A dark-haired man in casual khaki slacks and a short sleeve green golf shirt stood on the edge of the runway just behind the red security line. He waited patiently, slowly tapping his toe as he watched Matt and the chief take the time to say goodbye to the aircrew. The man repeatedly checked his watch while the SEAL platoon's leaders gave additional instructions to Boone and the other SEALs on where to stage the weapons and communications gear.

"It looks like the welcome wagon has arrived!" Boone noted, tilting his head in the direction of the stranger.

Matt and the chief turned to check out the company. Even at this short distance the mirage caused by the heat danced about the man's legs. Chief Auger placed his arms across his chest and stared at the waiting stranger.

"Well boss, let's see what the man's got on his mind," he said.

"Yeah, okay, Chief," Matt replied. "I think Boone's got a handle on things here. Let's go see what this trip is all about."

The two SEALs casually walked over to the gentleman. Matt extended his hand and smiled. No use pissing this guy off yet, he thought. The man returned Matt's smile but it didn't come off quite right.

"Welcome to Siganella, LT Barrett. I hope your flight was comfortable."

Matt looked at the chief before answering. "Well it was ok I guess. I take it you've never spent any time in a cargo plane, Mister…?"

"Oh yes, I'm sorry! My name is Stewart Jackson. I'm a cultural affairs officer with, shall we say, a rather small department of the U.S. government. I specialize in geography. In particular, North Africa."

Stewart reached out to shake Chief Auger's hand. "I hope our work together will be successful."

Chief Auger glanced at Matt and then erupted. "Come on, sir! I'm too damn old to play these stupid reindeer games! I've got a platoon of pissed off SEALs over there who want to know what the hell's going on around here! We were recalled from our homes in the middle of the night back in Virginia and ordered to load out for Siganella in twenty-four hours. As usual, their families and girlfriends don't know if the job is real this time or just a silly exercise. They also don't know if we'll be gone a week or a month. We aren't used to being fed shit and kept in the dark like mushrooms! So get to the point!"

Stewart Jackson had moved back a step or two during the chief's angry speech. Catching himself, he tried to stand a little taller and narrowed his eyes before responding.

"I assure you my intention is not to play games, chief. I need to brief the lieutenant so that he can start planning how you will handle the challenge that now lies before you. As soon as he reads the mission situation you'll understand why you've been kept in the dark."

Matt's eyes focused on the office geek in front of him.

"My chief is the brains of this outfit, Mr. Jackson. And I don't make decisions without his guidance and feedback. If you're here to give a mission brief, you'll damn well have to give it to both of us!"

The analyst's shock was plain to see on his face. He appeared taken aback by the intensity of Matt's comments. He must have assumed the enlisted SEALs just took orders and carried them out, and it never dawned on him they might actually be involved in evaluating mission assignments. He seemed to choose his words carefully before he answered.

"As you wish lieutenant. I don't have a problem briefing both of you. However, we do need to get to a secure location fairly soon so I can bring you, I mean both of you, up to speed on the mission."

Matt smiled in mocking victory. "Well, I do insist, Mr. Jackson. So sure, let's hit the road!"

A glance back showed him the guys were on autopilot unloading the plane.

"Chief, let Boone know we'll be out of pocket for a while. Don't let him in on what we're doing. Just have him carry the ball until the guys are settled."

"What about liberty for the boys?" the chief asked.

Matt paused to consider the request. "Well, Mr. Jackson, do my boys have time to unwind tonight?"

The agency man thought for a second. What harm could there be in letting the SEALs go out for one evening?

"Yes, yes of course, LT Barrett. You can tell your men it's okay to let their hair down so to speak. I mean, what could possibly happen in one night?"

The chief winked knowingly at Matt. "Yeah, boss. What could possibly happen in just one evening?"

"Nothing we can't handle. Right chief?"

Chief Auger nodded back. "That's affirmative, LT!"

With that, the chief turned and walked toward the SEALs working near the cargo plane. His concern over why they were here was growing by the minute. There ain't no good deals for SEALs when SEALs start hanging around company spooks, the chief mused. Matt watched the chief for a moment then turned back to the agency man impatiently rocking back and forth in front of him. Matt didn't like this guy. Not one bit. He decided it was better to stay detached until he knew what this was all about.

Within minutes the chief was back, giving Matt the thumbs up. Many career military types in the army and marines ridiculed the SEALs for their apparent lack of discipline and military bearing. However, when they had the opportunity to actually observe the navy's finest in action, they were puzzled by the way the enlisted frogmen seemed to work together with precision, requiring little or no direct guidance.

The simple fact was SEALs rarely gave any outward appearance of operating under classic military order and direction. That was because every man in a SEAL unit knew what the objective was and was personally committed to the successful completion of that objective. They didn't need some officer or NCO convincing them to care about the mission. When SEALs worked, they worked hard. Hence, another of the chief's favorite sayings, work hard–play hard!

The men of Matt's platoon were going to finish the off load. Then they were going to tear Siganella apart. Matt wasn't going to restrict their play tonight. Pity the SEAL officer who stands in the way of well-earned liberty time.

Matt kept that in mind as he and the chief piled into the dark agency sedan. Whatever the mission ahead, the boys deserved time to blow off some steam. Who knows? Maybe some of them would never have an opportunity like this again.

Matt tossed his briefcase on the bed. He was bushed from the long trip but felt the need to stretch his muscles. He changed into running shorts and a t-shirt and headed downstairs.

The base was flat and plain, nothing to look at really. Then Matt turned a corner and spotted the dominating dome of a dormant volcano. The aircraft departed and arrived like clockwork as Matt continued his circuit. His legs were feeling better now. The run was a good idea, cleared his mind too. Matt saw a sign for the base gym and cut his run short. Time to hit the weights.

CHAPTER EIGHT

The pounding wouldn't stop. Matt clutched the pillow tighter around his head and curled into a little ball. It seemed to help. As he drifted away again, a deep booming voice cut through his foggy mind. "Get the hell up and answer the damn door, sir!"

Matt uncurled and bolted upright, balancing on the edge of the bed, is violent reaction nearly kept him headed for the floor. His eyes snapped to the right. The clock read eight o'clock in the morning. "Oh shit, oh shit I'm late!"

He jumped off the bed and kept on going, his sock covered feet skating across the hand polished, parquet floor. Matt lost his balance and despite his flailing arms, gracelessly landed on his ass with a loud thump!

The pounding on the door started up again, but this time Matt couldn't ascertain if it was the door or between his ears. As the fuzziness cleared, he checked his wristwatch against the alarm clock and realized he'd screwed up big time. The loud voice sliced through his mental analysis with another demand to open the door. This time Matt could hear other voices in the hallway outside.

The naval officer unlocked and opened the door to see Chief Auger and Boone standing in the hall. The bachelor's quarters used local Sicilian cleaning ladies to keep the temporary quarters livable. One such elderly employee was now blankly staring at the SEALs. Just down the hall a younger American woman, probably a dependent spouse was ushering a small red headed boy into their room as quickly as possible. Everybody was staring at Matt.

"Shit!" Matt glanced down, then up, then back down again. He jumped backwards, removing his naked body from the hallway, and kicked the door shut.

"Our fearless leader rises!" Chief Auger laughed loudly at his own joke. The cleaning lady apparently understood English fairly well, because she got the point right away and began blushing.

"Come on, Boone, let's get the boss in the shower! We're going to need him in prime shape today."

Boone nodded and entered Matt's room. "Hey, chief, how do they pick guys to be officers anyhow?"

The older man turned and chuckled. "I'm not sure, buddy. But when you find out, let me know, okay?"

Boone just smiled and visually surveyed the trashed room. Maybe this guy wasn't so bad after all. The chief and Boone helped Matt into the bathroom and started the shower. Matt was shoved roughly into the booth. The cold water flowed over Matt, helping to clear his aching head. He couldn't believe he'd missed a platoon muster.

The briefing the day before had confirmed their earlier decision to let the platoon have a night on the town. The chief had suggested that Matt also try to relax a bit after the briefing, inviting him to join him for a few drinks. Once out, Chief Auger kept the rum and cokes flowing all night. Matt tried hard to remember if he'd actually saw the chief swallow any of the mixed drinks.

A classic tactic used by senior enlisted SEALs to slow down their energetic officers was to ambush them while on liberty. This normally occurred the night before a distasteful training event, or just to knock an officer's ego down a few notches. Unfortunately for Matt, if last night had been an ambush, he never saw it coming. The drill was simple; an officer was first surrounded by friendly SEAL enlisted men. Once in position these fine fellows proceeded to pour compliments and words of praise over their witless but fearless leader. Then one of the men would propose a toast to the platoon, or to the navy, or their mother.

Whatever the toast, a bottle of some dreadful mix would miraculously appear along with enough glasses for everyone. The officer would be so disarmed by the warmth and affection of his men that he gladly joined in the event. The tactics continued to evolve as the night wore on. One such tactic was known as the one on one drill. Over the course of an hour or so, an officer would be approached to discuss some personal issue of great importance with one of his enlisted SEALs. The enlisted man always arrived for his audience with a full can of beer or glass of some potion which was gracefully received by the empathetic officer.

After a while a roving pair of SEALs would crash in on the counseling session to propose a friendly toast. Of course they just happened to be carrying an extra shot glass. On average it would take the platoon about two hours to render the officer incapacitated. For obvious reasons the scheduled next morning event would be postponed or canceled while the men quietly tiptoed around the sleeping officer's room.

In Matt's case, the chief wasn't in on the fun and games. He had no idea that the night before the boys in the platoon had effectively and efficiently snookered their officer. The objective was to gain another day of liberty in Siganella before settling down to conduct training or work. Of course, the men didn't have a clue as to the real purpose of their presence in Italy. They had no idea they had turned their leader into a shaking mess on the eve of a real mission.

Now the day was burning up rapidly and Matt was severely behind the power curve. He had to hurry up and brief the team so they could begin working up a plan of action for the upcoming mission. Matt dressed quickly, and without saying a word, left the bachelor's quarters with Boone and the chief in tow.

They all rode quietly in the back of a dark green Italian army van that wound its way back and forth on the narrow roads. Within thirty minutes they arrived at the secure briefing site. The secure facility was actually a NATO operations center that the SEALs were given access to through the courtesy of their new swim buddy Mr. Jackson.

The SEALs entered the spacious briefing auditorium through a set of guarded double steel doors. Matt walked down the stairs to a podium set up mid-stage, as the chief and the rest of the platoon found a place to sit down. Matt looked up at the rows of assembled men to see knowing smiles. Matt couldn't help smiling himself. He was now officially initiated in the nocturnal drinking tactics and tricks of the navy's finest.

Luckily, the chief had suggested getting this warning order brief together right after their briefing with Mr. Jackson had been completed the day before. The faces turned serious when Matt hit the overhead projector's display button. The machine splashed a topographic map of northeastern Egypt, twenty feet high on the screen behind him.

"Gents, this is not an exercise. The situation in Egypt has been deteriorating steadily now for three or four months. A rebel leader named Banadar has infiltrated the military to the point where it's only a matter of time before the Egyptian government rolls over."

Matt paused for effect. "The United States is going to invade Egypt within seventy-two hours. Our mission tasking is to infiltrate Egyptian territorial waters six to eight hours prior to the main invasion event. We are going to move without detection to the commercial airport in the coastal city of Alexandria. Once there, we are to conduct a cursory reconnaissance of the target, report on its status, and then standby to support the initial Ranger strike force as it takes over the airport."

Matt began to pour over the warning order details, assigning duties and tasks related to the logistics of movement to the mission area, as well as jobs associated with the planning and rehearsal phase. With only a few hours left, every detail had to be perfect the first time. Most of the platoon's attention would be spent on the chalk talk. Sitting together debating the hundreds of possible outcomes of each and every action taken by the SEALs throughout every phase of the mission in Egypt.

Every man had a right and a duty to bring up any concerns or ideas he might have that could help ensure mission success. For the next two days Matt and his SEALs poured over Mr. Jackson's detailed target folder containing the Egyptian naval, ground, and air order of battle. They analyzed topographic guidance on preferred routes of infiltration and exfiltration. They also reviewed a mix of signals intelligence, CIA estimates, and general background information from mostly public sources, discussing Egypt and her people. The gaping hole in the assessments was a lack of any accurate data related to the force strength on and around the target itself.

On the face of it, Sparrow Hawk was a simple operation if American forces could just go in and escort U.S. citizens and European non-combatants out of harm's way. It would be a completely different animal to conduct an evacuation while fighting the Egyptian armed forces. The initial planning was straight forward enough. Matt's platoon would rely on SEAL standard operating procedures or SOPs, to execute virtually all aspects of the mission except actions on target.

Every SEAL mission was unique because every target situation was unique. The airport mission wasn't that difficult a task on the face of it. However, SEALs were not that good at predicting the future. Many times in the elite unit's illustrious past the SEALs found themselves on a target that should have been given to some other conventional unit, but instead had been given to the lightly armed frogmen.

Time flew by as the platoon struggled to cover all the logistics and tactical issues at hand. Matt and Chief Auger continued to mentally check off the primary concerns as they were addressed and resolved. First and foremost was the safety of his SEALs. His responsibility for them had been the driving force behind the rigorous training conducted by the platoon back in the States. Matt believed that the harder they trained, the more likely each of them would react correctly and therefore survive combat.

Matt also reviewed his personal responsibilities as a leader. He was, of course, a product of the same combat training as his men, so he felt personally ready for combat. He knew that enlisted SEALs did not tolerate weak officers. They quietly demanded that their officers at least keep up with them, and even better, excel at all the skills of the water warrior.

The platoon finally felt it had a firm grasp of the mission tasking. Matt knew the objective area like it was his old neighborhood. The communications package was simple yet functional. One thing SEALs hated was overbearing supervision via the radio. It was far too easy for higher commanders to micro-manage the mission remotely. Matt made sure the command and control network supporting the mission was adequate but not heavy handed. The communications were lean, but Matt didn't want to have to lug any more radios around than were absolutely necessary.

Matt's thoughts were interrupted when Chief Auger placed his hand on the lieutenant's shoulder. "Well boss, the boys look real sharp. I wouldn't run them through rehearsals again unless you see something I don't see."

Matt tilted his head in the chief's direction. "Yeah, I think you're right, chief. We'll let the guys take a break for a while. I don't want them to peak too early. Let's get the parachutes packed up and the mission equipment staged at the hangar before we cut them loose."

"You got it, LT!" the chief agreed. Hey LT, something chewing on you? The lights are on but it don't look like anybody's home."

Matt looked right at the chief and smiled. "No chief, I'm as ready as I'll ever be. Go ahead and get the guys moving. I'll catch up with you later. Oh yeah, no liberty tonight, that also means no beer in the barracks, understood?"

"Sure thing boss, I'm rolling right now!" The chief trotted over to the assembled SEALs to put the word out. Matt watched him move away.

He felt lucky to have such a great chief. Matt knew this would have been a lot more difficult without Chief Auger's experience and guidance. Matt tried hard but couldn't think of anything he'd missed. He knew from his training experience that second-guessing his decisions would be counter productive.

This whole thing was just so different from conducting routine training. He couldn't help imagining any number of disasters. The flashback of himself as a young SEAL LTJG struggling to cross a road was a common theme. He also couldn't stop thinking about his dad. Was he sitting up there somewhere watching the show? I bet he's already predicted I'll fail, Matt mused. The old man might have been able to handle a job like this without a hitch. But then again Arthur Barrett had never been a SEAL.

Matt refocused once again. He felt he should spend a little more time on the geography of the emergency exfiltration route since the terrain was so different from the built up urban area around the airport. He considered it for a second and then decided to blow it off. Matt needed a break. He was sure he could cross that bridge when he came to it.

CHAPTER NINE

Washington D.C.–White House situation room

The duty officer nodded while listening to the flash telephone report. The American embassy in Cairo was forwarding their interpretation of the most recent act of terrorism. The crowds of European and American tourists were always large this time of year. So the devastation wrought by the large blast near the pyramid of Giza efficiently struck down one hundred and twelve people within a few seconds.

The duty officer took detailed notes during the phone call. He was responsible for logging the information prior to forwarding it to his superior. Just when he thought the report was finished, the embassy staffer's voice on the other end raised to a high pitch. He began a new report. This new data, the duty officer knew, was very sensitive and would have to be passed up the chain of command immediately.

The call ended abruptly. The White House duty officer stared at the dead receiver in his hand for a second before pressing the button to connect him with the communications officer in the basement below. Before attempting to reconnect with Egypt he turned to a military aide standing close by.

"Captain! Take this note to General Hawkins. He's down the hall speaking with the national security advisor. Interrupt them and tell them I consider the content of the note to be of immediate operational interest!"

The captain saluted and rushed out of the room. The duty officer now picked up the phone and dialed the switchboard.

"Have you been able to get through to our embassy in Egypt?"

"No sir! We've tried to patch through every way we know how and we can't get through to Cairo."

The duty officer was confused. "Do you mean to say all the lines at the Embassy are busy?" The reply came immediately.

"No sir, I'm saying that all communication with the embassy has been cut off at the source."

The impact of these words stunned the duty officer. How could the embassy's communications capability be interrupted? The U.S. embassy in Cairo was a state-of-the-art communications station. Hell, the facility had more broadcast capability than the host country! His thoughts were abruptly cut short by the noisy arrival of General Hawkins, JCS duty officer at the White House.

"Dan! What do you make of this report? Is it possible that both the Egyptian air force and the Egyptian army have rolled over to that madman Banadar?"

The duty officer turned to face the general squarely. "Sir, not only is it true, but I have reason to believe our embassy in Cairo may be under direct or indirect attack even as we speak."

General Hawkins looked shaken for a moment. Then his face transformed as resolve took hold. "Dan, go get the national security advisor and ask him politely to come down here. Don't go into great detail, but tell him enough for him to realize his presence is urgently required. Then call the JCS desk at the Pentagon and have them initiate a code blue recall. When you have that rolling, call European command and exchange information. Oh yeah, if they haven't already done so, have them contact Admiral Carden at Sixth Fleet in Italy and tell them to standby for execution of that Egypt plan. What was it called?"

"Sparrow Hawk sir, Operation Sparrow Hawk."

Hangar Thirty Five–Siganella, Sicily

They were running out of time. The schedule had just been moved up by twelve hours. Matt looked around the aircraft hangar as each member of the team made their final preparations in their own private way. The SEALs had determined the best method of insertion without detection, was by air. The chief was putting the finishing touches on the flight plan, manipulating the laptop navigation console's controls to confirm all the various course legs were inputted correctly.

The console's computer would allow the primary navigator during the high altitude—high opening, or HAHO, flight to make best use of the prevailing winds at different altitudes during the team's descent. Once the men jumped off the tail ramp the HAHO technique would allow the SEALs to descend under specially designed parachutes, riding the winds as if traveling down a series of escalators.

The insertion aircraft shared the hangar with them. The MH-53 PAVLOW special operations helicopter loomed over everything in the small space. The impressive array of weapons and antennae gave the twenty-five foot long helicopter a sinister, business like appearance. The elite air force aircrew members tinkered here and there, trying to make efficient use of the little remaining time before mission takeoff.

Matt knew the aircrews could be counted on to do everything right. The air force PAVLOW helicopters had been the first aircraft to enter Iraqi airspace and initiate the massive air campaign in Operation Desert Storm. Their unique electronics package included state-of-the-art electronic jamming and electronic counter measures systems. They were the very best in the world at what they did.

The helicopter crew chief passed Matt and held up his hands. He showed all ten fingers and then made two fists. He repeated this once more before moving on to the aircraft nearby. Matt understood. Only twenty minutes until wheels up. It was time to get the guys together. Matt yelled over to the chief to round up the team. He then gathered up his personal equipment and moved over to the pre-selected jock up point.

The term jock up was taken from the early days of navy deep sea diving. When divers put on the heavy canvas and brass suits, it required everybody's assistance. The SEALs were all combat divers first and the phrase aptly communicated the need for teamwork as each SEAL donned his mission equipment and HAHO rig.

The boys were all lined up at the tail ramp ahead of him. Matt could see they were anxious to get rolling. However, the seriousness of the event was not lost on any of them, they were still warriors, and warriors lived for this kind of shit.

Matt smiled at the faces all around him. "Okay, gentlemen, you know the deal. Let's go over it one more time. Boone, run down the checklist until we're under canopy."

"Yes sir!" Boone's voice was all business as he covered the suit-up procedures. As the platoon's jumpmaster, he was responsible for final equipment and parachute checks prior to embarking the Helo. "You guys get first checks from the LT right over there."

Boone pointed to a spot near the back of the Helo. "Then I want you each to get final checks from me at the ramp. Everyone will enter the bird in reverse order of the exit plan. Go as far forward on the starboard side as possible. Make sure you have all your shit with you, we ain't making any Seven-Eleven runs if you leave stuff behind!"

This last comment brought a chuckle from the assembled jumpers. Boone continued. "We'll be executing a tail ramp exit, jumping off the green light. I'll go first followed by each of you in your assigned order. The LT will be last man out. We have a ninety-minute flight to the drop point. Exit altitude will be at fifteen thousand feet. Expect to be under canopy by thirteen thousand. As usual, muster on the low man and tighten the formation up as soon as possible. You guys know the drill, so let's start this show off right. The LT and I will discuss any problems over the headsets but everyone else, stay off the net unless it's an emergency. I guess that's it, LT, it's not like we haven't done this a few hundred times before!"

Matt nodded. "Good job, Boone, thorough as usual. Chief, I want you to go over the mission phases one last time."

The chief grunted in reply and faced the group. He just caught the eye of the helicopter crew checking their watches and shaking their heads. "Alright guys I'll make this short and sweet. Boone covered phase one pretty well. Phase two begins when our flight formation hits the water. If Boone's navigation is any good, we will be fifty to one hundred yards off the insertion beach. Get out of your harness and swim away from it. The weights in the harness pockets will take that crap straight to the bottom and out of sight. The team will muster together and get a good head count. Don't forget to put a few puffs of air into your life vest to compensate for all the mission gear."

Matt checked his watch and gave Chief Auger the signal to speed up the briefing review. The chief nodded.

"We'll swim in, four to a side in a parallel column toward the beach landing site. Boone and Jorgy will detach to recon the beach. The rest of us will buddy up. One man covering the recon team while his partner takes his fins off. When the first guy's ready to go, switch roles. Boone will signal us if the beach looks okay using a flashing red alpha code. That's dit-dah for you bone heads! Once the LT gives us the thumbs-up, the rest of us will leapfrog ashore two at a time. We'll set up a perimeter near the high water line, then wait and listen for a while before moving inland. You have anything to add LT?"

"Yeah chief, remember we need to send the feet dry codeword by UHF burst transmission before we move out. So, Boone, you need to wait for my thumbs up."

"Roger that, boss," Boone responded.

The chief continued his part of the briefing. "That ends phase two. Phase three is the patrol to the airport. We just need to stick to the time line and avoid contact. Remember, a firefight is probable cause for a mission abort. So keep your eyes and ears open. We will adhere to standard patrol procedures and deal with any surprises based on our SOPs. Phase four covers our actions on target. Our mission task is to conduct reconnaissance and surveillance of the airport. We have purposefully kept this part of the phase loose and flexible. Our final actions on target are to assist the Ranger's raid on the airport if possible. Now we aren't going to get in a fistfight trying to help the Rangers. They can take care of themselves. But we can help spot targets for the air support guys. Let's stick to what we know. Keep it simple. You guys all know what happened at Patilla airport in Panama in 1989. The name of the game is stealth all the way on this one."

The men all knew about the heavy casualties experienced by SEAL team four during the U.S. invasion of Panama. Four SEALs had died and many more were severely wounded trying to disable President Noriega's private jet. The mission ran into severe trouble when the rigid SEAL plan fell apart in the rapidly changing environment.

Although the mission was considered a critical military success, the SEAL community was left in a state of shock because of the heavy losses. Nobody in this platoon wanted to achieve success at that price. The chief pressed on with the briefing.

"Phase five is patrol movement to our primary extraction point near the airport if something goes wrong with the Ranger raid. Of course, if the Rangers complete their task at the airport successfully, we'll be riding back in style, courtesy of the U.S. Army! You guys need to keep thinking about what ifs, and be flexible at all times. We are very good at what we do. That, and teamwork will get us through this operation. That's all I've got, LT!"

"Thanks, chief. Remember men, the first casualty upon contact with the enemy will probably be the plan, so we'll stick to what we rehearsed, as long as it fits. As soon as the shit hits the fan we'll just have to use our heads and our firepower to give us some thinking room. Any questions?"

Wells raised his hand. "Yeah, I mean, yes sir, what are the chances these army guys don't show up at all? You know, get lost or something stupid like that?"

Matt waited for the laughter to abate. "Don't worry, Wells, I think this time will be different."

Most SEALs knew the track record established from previous special operations missions in Grenada and Panama. During the invasion of Grenada, SEALs waited under fire for twenty plus hours for a relief force that was supposed to take over the target one hour after the invasion began. The same thing happened again in Panama. Attacking SEALs were denied MEDEVAC and fire support assets during early firefights in the capital city. To add insult to injury, the marine force assigned to link-up at Paitilla airfield on the first night never arrived.

Wells' response was cut off by a high-pitched whine coming from just outside the hangar door. The platoon looked towards the sound. The crew chief motioned energetically for the team to board the SPECOPS bird. Matt waved back to acknowledge the crewman's signal.

"Okay guys, this is it! Let's load-up!"

The platoon broke up, each man grabbing his helmet and goggles. Matt and the enlisted SEALs walked stiffly to the tail ramp. They quickly organized themselves and, as briefed by Chief Auger, began to enter the aircraft in reverse order. The aircrew completed their final checks and confirmed each SEAL was safely belted in. With the team securely seated inside the bird, a crewmember pressed a button that lifted the tail ramp to its full raised position for flight. Within seconds the helicopter rose slowly into the night sky. As it passed the tail end of the runway, all of the aircraft's lights blinked out. Operation Sparrow Hawk was underway.

CHAPTER TEN

There was nothing quite like it. The powerful blast of cold air at twenty thousand feet sharpened Matt's senses. It was always a thrill for him to watch the tail ramp open in preparation for a jump. And there were few things Matt enjoyed more in life than the thrill of leaping into open space.

The first time Matt jumped out of a perfectly good airplane had been at Army jump school. All BUD/S graduates reported to Fort Benning, Georgia enroute to their first SEAL command. The course was designed for regular Army volunteers. And when the freshly minted SEALs hit the base all hell broke loose!

Matt and his fellow SEALs participated in the not so rigorous physical training while learning the art of parachuting. All SEALs were required to graduate from Fort Benning after the standard five jumps. Matt thought the first jump would be the worst but it was the second jump that took real guts to get through.

All five jumps at Fort Benning were static line jumps. This technique was virtually unchanged from the days of World War Two. A jumper wore a harness with a round parachute folded and packed into a rectangular pack. A nylon cord was attached to the back of the pack. This "static line" was then hooked onto a wire cable in the jump aircraft.

When the jumper stepped out of the aircraft, the static line went taut and his body weight ripped the back of the pack open, deploying the parachute. Matt was happy the SEALs focused on advanced parachute techniques such as HAHO. He hated the concept of hanging from a rope.

Matt re-focused his attention on the men in his platoon. They were as ready as they could be considering the limited time allowed them. He knew that this jump was the most fragile of the various mission phases. He and the other SEALs had to rely on the skill of the aircrew to get them to the right exit point. An exit error of only a few thousand yards could translate into mission failure. Even worse, his platoon could wind up floating in the middle of the Med.

The red light mounted near the ramp door changed to green. The eight man platoon moved to the ramp smoothly and exited as briefed, with Boone as the heaviest going first and Matt, as team leader, going last. Falling from a helicopter was a little different than jumping from a fixed wing airplane. The MH-53 PAVLOW created minimal down draft with its one multi-blade rotor, compared to the powerful jet or turbo prop storm generated by many standard jump aircraft. Once out of the helicopter it took a few more seconds for the SEALs to stabilize their bodies in free fall.

Boone was responsible for wearing and operating the laptop navigation console and as the first man out he fell the farthest before pulling his rip chord. The rest of the platoon was required to stay within three yards of each other. If things were done correctly, they would stack directly above and behind the man in front of them.

Each SEAL muttered a different delay count before opening his chute. This allowed the group to create an initial dead space between them. This dead space had to be maintained while flying under canopy. The hundreds of practice jumps over the last year paid off as each chute popped open with a loud cracking sound. The expertise of the SEALs was evident by the near perfect stair step column formed by their canopies.

Matt looked down and counted the chutes before reporting into his throat mike.

"Head count is complete!"

Now that the team was assembled, Boone could now stop circling and proceed on the first leg of the course. He glanced at his laptop navigation console and gently pulled down on his left steering toggle. The night air was dry and becoming warmer with every foot of the platoon's descent. Each man was no further than six feet away from the man in front of and just below him in formation. They were each guided in the dark by colored light panels mounted on each of their parachute harnesses. Red on the right, green on the left. Match them up and you knew the guy in front of you was flying away, not at you. It was all the control they needed as long as they stayed close.

Boone executed his second turn and steadied up on a new course for the second leg of the aerial journey. He would continue to ride the wind line until reaching a predetermined drop in altitude before shifting course again to a new wind line. The flight computer calculated these courses so the SEALs could take advantage of the prevailing tail winds and descend as if walking down a series of stairs pointing in different directions. Once they were below five thousand feet, however, the ride became much simpler. Boone would try to maximize the team's altitude so they'd have more height rather than less when they arrived offshore. If he brought them in too low, they would be forced to land far out to sea, resulting in a long swim.

The platoon continued its descent without incident. At two thousand feet Boone began to lazily swing left and right in order to eat up altitude. At one thousand feet he picked his landing point in the ocean and aimed directly for it. The lights of Alexandria shown like a bowl of polished diamonds. The outline of the great breakwater that once held Cleopatra's palace was just off to their left. Looking out at the beautiful sight, it was hard for Matt to believe this wasn't just a training operation.

The team stayed tight until the last few feet, the final approach. Just prior to contact with the ocean, each man jammed his steering toggles down hard to stall his chute right over Boone's entry point into the water. As air dumped out of the canopy, it stopped any forward movement and dropped the SEAL straight into the water. The platoon was in enemy territorial waters now and there was no going back. The arrival of the armed American SEALs was an act of war.

Pentagon Situation Room–Washington, D.C.

The air force major glanced up when he heard the high-pitched sound. The audio alarm indicated receipt of another phase execution codeword for Operation Sparrow Hawk. So far the status boards concerning phase one of the operation displayed positive initial reports by all air related infiltration phases. The major looked for and found the source of the alarm on checklist three, the Green Beret HALO team had signaled its arrival feet dry in Egypt. Their team's mission was to seize an important radio relay site, override the system, and begin broadcasting soothing propaganda to the Egyptian people.

A second alarm went off. The major glanced across the various boards until he spotted the new update. The SEALs were feet wet. The codeword SPLASH explained it well enough. Now things were really going to start hopping around here, he thought. Another alarm kicked off.

The Egyptian Coastline

The water was warm and salty. Especially if you swallowed some, which is exactly what Matt did while struggling out of his MT-1X parachute harness. Nearby he heard the grunting and sputtering of someone else suffering the same fate. Matt took a quick head count. So far, so good. The team was bobbing just thirty yards offshore. Boone had completed a brilliant job of navigating the fourth and final leg of their flight to put them smack dab in the area between the beach and the crushing surf zone. The constant booming of the breaking waves seemed to help increase Matt's confidence in his early decision to HAHO infiltrate instead of using the SDV or CRRCs.

Matt looked around for Wells. He spotted him with his head down near Jorgy. Before he could say anything, Wells winked, giving Matt a thumbs-up signal. Matt smiled back at the radioman and returned the signal. Wells had already sent the feet wet codeword via a secure waterproof UHF radio. Wells put the hand-held communications device away and waited for the next move. Matt turned away to get yet one more head count. He needed to stop worrying about the men and start leading the mission.

Egyptian Air Base Outside Cairo

Banadar uncrossed his legs, pushing himself off the floor with one smooth motion. It was obvious that the leaders of Egypt's proud military services weren't used to sitting on the floor. They each had to roll around a little before struggling to their feet. Their concern for their appearance was comical. They each took time to fuss with their uniforms until they were satisfied with their appearance. If any of these swollen pigs survive this revolution, Banadar mused, I will enjoy making them re-learn the hard ways of their desert ancestors.

Banadar stood to one side, quietly acknowledging each officer as they left the room. But his thoughts were far away. Running over the final steps in his grand maneuver, Banadar was now fairly certain everything was ready and in place. In fact, the first exercise of his new power would take place within hours. The action would signal the beginning of the end for the tyrants, and like a sudden desert wind, usher in a new beginning for his people.

Banadar walked outside he stopped for a moment then looked up into the clear night sky. By morning the infidels would know that he and his followers were for real, and by morning the whole world would know that Egypt was free at long last!

Beach Landing Site–Egypt

Boone's flashing red "alpha" signal let the team know the immediate beach-landing site or BLS was clear. Matt couldn't see Boone and Cruise in the shadows along the high berm, but he knew they were there. It had taken all of twenty-eight minutes for the team to swim with great stealth to the water's edge and for the swimmer scout pair to complete its assigned task.

Without looking backwards, Matt pointed with his index finger toward the beach. Wells looked at the chief and they began crawling immediately. Two at a time, the SEALs moved quickly across the beach to join the swimmer scouts. As they arrived, each pair took up defensive positions addressing the flanks and inshore approaches. Since Jorgy had the M-60 machine gun, he was primarily responsible for responding to any attack while the team finished its transition from frogman to commando.

Doc and Oby were the last to join the perimeter on the beach. Matt watched as Wells transmitted the "feet dry" codeword via the UHF radio. As soon as Wells finished packing up the radio, Matt signaled Boone to kick the team into gear. Matt noticed he felt uncomfortably cold. Although they were in a desert country, the long process of getting to the BLS from Italy had sapped them all of energy. To make things worse, the human body continually perspired when placed under stress. So even though they had pre-hydrated prior to the flight, he was sure he wasn't the only one who had pissed away a pint or two during the ocean swim. All of the stress and perspiration had combined to create the onset of mild hypothermia.

Matt motioned for Boone to take them inland. Boone nodded slightly in response. He was all business as he unwound to his full height. The point man cautiously scanned the unknown terrain in front of him from left to right and back again. His movement was copied in kind by the others in the patrol, as the rest of the team stood up and looked to their individual fields of fire. They all knew the drill. The platoon had thousands of hours of patrolling practice behind it. However, this time it was different. This time it was real!

Chief Auger turned and signaled for Doc to get Oby's attention. The chief knew from experience that frequently SEAL rear security men would be so intent on looking backwards they would be left behind when the patrol moved out. Oby turned when tapped by Doc, nodded, and got to his feet. Matt watched his rear security for a moment then turned his attention forward again. He didn't think anyone was going to sleep on this operation.

The SEALs fell into their standard file order. Boone at point was responsible for navigation to the target and contact reaction forward. Matt, as patrol leader, was positioned behind Boone and slightly ahead of Jorgy and his big machine gun. Matt's field of fire was to the right because Jorgy's M-60 was belt fed. This meant Jorgy had to point his weapon to the left in order to operate it properly. By keeping twice the distance away from Jorgy, Matt and Boone created a separate two-man point element.

Wells followed Jorgy and carried the team's communications equipment. He also carried a short model A-2 carbine with a M-203 grenade launcher attached under the rifle's barrel. His field of fire was to the right. In addition to the SATCOM radio, Wells carried a primary and a back up UHF hand held radios to control U.S. aircraft, special marking beacons, and panels for use in marking landing zones and airstrips to support MEDEVAC of casualties or emergency team extraction.

The first four men in the patrol were designated fire team one. Cruise was the first SEAL in fire team two, right behind Wells. His job was to maintain the pace count. By counting every step of his left foot Cruise could calculate when the SEALs had covered a distance of one hundred meters. He then marked the distance by sliding a black bead down a rawhide string tied to his combat vest. Every thousand meters, or one kilometer traveled, was passed up to the LT via hand signals.

This old Ranger trick was simple and effective. By passing the information up and down the patrol in this manner, all the SEALs were kept aware of their current position. In addition, at each temporary halt Matt and the chief would show each fire team where the patrol was on the map and indicate the location of the closest emergency linkup point. If separated due to contact with the enemy, the SEALs would move as pairs, groups, or individually if necessary back to the last designated rendezvous point. Cruise also carried specially rigged anti-personnel mines called claymores, in addition to his silenced German MP-5SD submachine gun.

SEALs have always had a love affair with the claymore mine and they were especially gifted at modifying the devices to suit their needs. The SEALs usually primed the back of the weapon with very short lengths of time fuse. When a SEAL patrol was being pursued, these "stay behind" devices could be set up quickly to cover their retreat. Anybody running up behind them would suddenly eat six hundred steel ball bearings traveling at subsonic speed as the short time fuse set off the device. The claymore mine was so devastating it could easily take out four to five enemy soldiers in one whack. Cruise carried five mines.

Chief Auger followed Cruise in the line of march. As assistant patrol leader or APL, he was responsible for taking head counts and conducting backup navigation. He would also take command of the team when Matt and Boone went off to scout around. The chief carried extras of everything; two claymores, compression bandages, radio batteries and various items only a man of his operational experience would appreciate.

He also carried a silenced MP-5 SD submachine gun. The chief and Cruise were also assigned to pair up and be responsible for quiet elimination of sentries and silent room entry. Chief Auger's field of fire was to the right, opposite that of Cruise.

Doc was next in line. Doc carried a field surgery bag and every kind of bandage imaginable. The first SEAL on the scene handled initial response to trauma. Each man was a graduate of advanced trauma care and qualified to start an IV to prepare a wounded comrade for MEDE-VAC. Doc had made up "blowout kits" for each man to carry.

These kits consisted of an IV, morphine, and one medium sized battle dressing. The SEALs in Matt's platoon all kept their blowout kits in an extra M-16 magazine pouch attached to their equipment belt. The kits were designed to quickly stop bleeding and stabilize a wounded man until Doc could look them over. Doc's job as team medic was to guide the work of others and attend to any extreme injury that existed such as amputation or life threatening chest wounds.

Historically when a man was hit his swim buddy reacted before the corpsman even knew there was a problem. The SOP was to use the wounded man's med gear not yours. Same thing applied when using water to clean the wound. If this procedure wasn't followed, your personal load out would depart with the wounded SEAL as he was flown out via MEDEVAC helicopter, leaving you on the ground with less water and an empty med kit. Often times it was a machine gunner or rear security who saved your life. Coincidentally, many of the SEAL corpsman evolved into the most adept killers in the deployed platoons.

Doc carried the A-2 carbine with M-203 grenade launcher. He and Matt were responsible for hauling and employing forty-millimeter illumination and signaling flares. Doc's field of fire was to the left. Finally there was Oby. Oby brought up the tail end as rear security and was responsible for checking the SEALs trail to detect any evidence of enemy trackers or pursuit.

He carried a breakdown fifty-caliber sniper rifle in a soft case strapped diagonally across his back and a German MP-5SD sub machine gun. Oby could be teamed up with Boone for long scouting trips where Matt felt like sticking with the team. He of course was used as the stand off weapons expert and could be paired up with any other SEAL. Usually in this mode, Oby and his partner would find a high observation point and control movement in a large area. He was the last SEAL in fire team two. The patrol moved quietly and easily over the rolling Egyptian terrain.

Each man's eyes moving in coordination with his weapon, the environment was about what the SEALs had expected, windy, dry and uninhabited. The low scrub all around stood about four to five feet tall. This was somewhat of a surprise—the overhead photography misrepresented their height substantially. The SEAL platoon swept their weapons back and forth smoothly to fully cover their assigned field of fire in a menacing ballet of death.

The SEALs patrolled for forty-five minutes, covering ground at a good pace. Matt's early chill was rapidly replaced with sweat as the exertion of walking over the broken ground in the dark took its toll. It felt good to be finally approaching the target, Matt thought. The long rehearsal and briefing process always seemed to take the adventure and thrill out of the job by over thinking and over planning every aspect of the mission. Now, here on Egyptian soil, it seemed like something wild and exciting again.

Matt wondered for the first time in a long time, just what would Dad think of all this? Matt could envision the old man sitting up in heaven somewhere, probably in a lawn chair, with a few marine buddies. His dad would critique the hell out of the mission, betting that Matt would surely screw things up. Well, Dad, Matt thought, it ain't over til it's over!

He knew he had until dawn to pull this deal off. Just make it to dawn and go home safe. The time flew by without incident. After patrolling tactically for an hour and a half, Matt could see the lights of downtown Alexandria ahead. That meant they were a thirty-minute movement from their objective. They would have to be on their toes from here on in. Moving this close to the population increased the chances the platoon would be detected before reaching the airport.

Matt considered ordering a short water break. He didn't want the team to get fatigued and stumble into trouble. Boone's form just ahead of Matt disappeared, interrupting his train of thought. Without thinking about it, Matt's body reacted in kind, hitting the deck and rolling to the right.

Instinctively all the SEALs followed Boone's and Matt's example. The SEALs had practiced these contact drills over and over until they were able to execute them without verbal commands. Matt settled into his firing position next to Boone. Without speaking Boone had communicated a lot of critical information to the entire team. Whatever was ahead of them was a direct threat. Whoever they were they were apparently unaware of the SEALs.

The intruders were very close. Matt's quick glance to the left confirmed that the rest of the team was also in position facing the road. He was about to ask Boone what the hell was going on, when he heard the voices. A million thoughts rushed through Matt's mind as he frantically searched the darkness for the source of the sounds. The low bushes obstructed his view. He could barely even make out the outline of Boone's body nearby. Matt's heart pounded louder and louder. It seemed to get so loud he was sure the approaching men would hear it and compromise his team's hasty ambush.

The SEALs stayed perfectly still. As the voices grew louder, the men remained focused and in control. This was it! The Super Bowl and

World Series all rolled into one. They had each waited, what seemed a lifetime, to prove they had what it took to excel in combat with the enemy. The hasty ambush site was set and they had a good kill zone clearly defined by the roadbed in front of them. Matt and the others knew the mission imperative was not to get caught, to engage the enemy only if fired upon prior to arrival at the airport. So, if this turned out to be a regular patrol, they would hold their fire and let them pass safely. Regardless of their desire to attack the enemy, the mission must always come first.

Matt's wildly spinning thoughts quickly began to organize themselves. His training took over as he ran down his tactical checklist. Boone had not been spotted. And the team had reacted correctly to Boone's maneuver by forming the firing line on the edge of the road. They had an awesome array of firepower at their disposal and they had the element of surprise. If the visitors wanted to rumble—Matt and his fellow SEALs were ready to oblige. The SEAL hasty ambush was a simple action requiring the application of superior firepower brought to bear on a well-defined area or kill zone.

The platoon's firepower was balanced across the patrol in a pre-planned manner. Each SEAL was aware of exactly what to do if the shit hit the fan. The riflemen were responsible for individual targets. Jorgy and his machine gun would sweep the kill zone, spreading the devastating linked 7.62 rounds left to right and back again. Once each rifleman fired their aimed shots, they would also sweep their weapons left to right. The effect of all the SEAL weapons used in this overlapping manner increased the kill zone by five yards on each side and ensured that no one caught in the middle could survive.

The SEALs had always been masters of the ambush. In the swamps and jungles of Vietnam, they refined the battle technique to a fine art, often employing demolition devices and claymore anti-personnel mines to increase their firepower. One thing the Viet Cong learned the hard way, no one survived a SEAL ambush, ever!

CHAPTER ELEVEN

Matt heard the crunching of boots as the enemy soldiers on the road moved closer. He realized he was going to have to defer to the judgment of his men because he wasn't in a position to see the patrol. If the group walked by harmlessly, so be it. If not, if just one Egyptian soldier paused or looked at the roadside in a funny way, Matt knew one of his guys would take the initiative and open up.

He could see them now, just barely, the outline of the dark silhouettes moving past Boone. Matt estimated the distance between the SEALs and the Egyptians to be no more than five yards. In anticipation of a worst-case outcome, Matt applied pressure with his thumb on the M-16's fire selector switch. He realized he couldn't employ the M203 grenade launcher mounted underneath the barrel of his rifle. His launcher was loaded with forty millimeter HE, or high explosive rounds, great against men in the open, but useless at this close range.

Matt knew the chief and Doc were not carrying HE rounds but instead had special forty-millimeter loads similar to buck shot. The effect of these rounds on the human body was devastating. Each small pellet was the equivalent of a small caliber bullet. Fired at close range, the virtual cloud of lead would cut a man in half. Even a near miss would easily take off an arm or leg.

So far Matt was sure he had counted at least four men passing by his position. He needed to see what was happening! Matt was trying to shift his weight to get a better view when all hell broke loose. BOOM! BOOM! BRAAAP! Matt recognized the crashing signature created by the detonating claymore anti-personnel mines. He flinched as Jorgy's M—60 opened up right next to him. He hadn't realized Jorgy was so close.

Matt snapped out of it and took aim at a shape on the road. He fired two quick aimed shots before the shape disappeared, then yelled to the other SEALs, "Shift your fire lower! Aim at the road!"

Men throughout the modern age of warfare have learned the hard way that shooting high at night was instinctive and a complete waste of ammunition. People being shot at tend to hit the ground and stay flat. All the bullets in the world wouldn't achieve anything unless they are aimed down where the target was hiding after the initial volley of fire.

The Viet Cong had learned this lesson well and often escaped attack by overwhelming but ineffective American firepower by staying low and beating a hasty retreat. As Matt repeatedly shouted the command, the SEALs red tracer fire dropped lower to create a tight impact area defined by the road in front of them.

Matt observed that his men were sweeping their weapons effectively. The scene playing out before the frogmen was a wicked dance of light and sound. Although only fifteen seconds had elapsed since the SEALs attacked, it felt like hours.

Chief Auger was yelling. "Cease fire! Cease fire!"

Matt needed to end the ambush. It took only five seconds more for the shooting to die out. As the last pop echoed in the night, Matt barked out new commands. "Set security! Search team, in!"

Wells immediately twisted around and faced away from the road watching the dunes and covering their backside. Boone jumped out of his ambush position and took up a firing position facing the direction where the Egyptians had come from. Oby, as rear security, moved out onto the road and setup facing the opposite direction of Boone. Matt kept Jorgy close to him on the original firing line as Chief Auger, Doc, and Cruise moved out on a skirmish line to clear the kill zone.

"Fire in the hole!"

Cruise popped a round into an Egyptian soldier lying on the road. His body was curled away from the approaching search team, possibly hiding a poised weapon or grenade. Doc acted as cover man for the search effort as Chief Auger and Cruise checked, one by one, each of the other bodies. The soldiers were scattered about the road like clumps of old rags. Boone called out, "Thirty seconds!"

His job during an ambush was to keep track of how much time had elapsed since the firefight broke out. Pursuit in the form of reinforcements would eventually react to the noise of combat. Boone needed to ensure the platoon didn't overstay their welcome.

Chief Auger moved to Matt's side.

"Well Boss, the guys sure kicked some major ass! Not a scratch on any of us. And I've got a body count of twelve on the road!"

Matt stared at the dark shape next to him. Twelve? Twelve men dead in less than thirty seconds of sound and fury? "Chief, are we that good or just lucky?"

"These men are pros, Boss. They did their job! Luck didn't have a damn thing to do with it!"

Matt silently agreed with the chief's assessment. He wondered if Chief Auger ever got tired of babysitting officers.

The chief was trying to get Matt's attention.

"Hey LT, I think we need to move the bodies off the road and get the hell out of here!"

Matt stared at his chief. "Is that what you think we should do?"

"Yeah, that's what I think we should do, sir! Let's stop playing grab ass and get moving!"

Matt's senses were sharpening rapidly. The chief was right.

"Okay, chief. Let's maintain security until the road's clear and then form up on Boone over there." Matt pointed out where Boone lay on the road. The chief nodded without answering. He turned and walked quickly to where Wells was waiting.

The SEALs started tidying up the place, moving bodies off the road and policing up loose Egyptian equipment. Matt kneeled down and took out his red lens penlight. He studied a laminated, topographic map of the area. According to his calculations they were still a good twenty-minute tactical patrol from the airport. If they just walked the distance the time would be cut in half.

Matt moved aside the black wristband covering the luminous face of his navy issue dive watch. The SEALs were ten minutes behind schedule. Matt had a choice to make. Rush to the target and be in position to support the Sparrow Hawk reconnaissance objectives, or patrol properly and tactically, and by his reckoning arrive too late to provide timely intelligence data to the Ranger assault element coming in to hit the airport.

Matt looked around as the last of his men joined the defensive perimeter. The dark road appeared to be clear of any sign of the recent ambush. The dark pools of blood created by the dead were slowly soaking into the fine dirt covering the road. Matt slid toward Boone in the perimeter and waved for him to move closer.

"We need to get off this damn road, Boss!" Boone whispered through clinched teeth. "I figure we are behind the power curve by now. We need to move fast for ten minutes or so, then slow down and make a good final approach."

Matt thanked God that he had such great people to rely on. Boone had also been running the numbers. His idea had provided the team with a workable compromise for movement to the target.

Forty Nautical Miles Offshore–Alexandria, Egypt

The young Rangers huddled together in the large aircraft checking and re-checking their individual equipment. The Air Force MH-53 PAVLOW helicopter was not only a great parachute platform but was also a unique special operations airframe designed to carry either cargo or troops into a hot combat landing zone. The helicopter also had other capabilities that went far beyond carrying men and supplies. It could jam enemy radar, sending a flood of deceptive electronic signals that simulated the radar signature of just about anything that flew.

Just one helicopter could make itself appear to enemy radar like a flight of B-52 bombers or a strike force of A-10 tank killers. The PAVLOWs also had sophisticated weapons systems. The highly trained crew controlled high technology lasers that could pinpoint stationary or moving targets on the ground, at night, and eliminate those targets with a number of deadly killing tools.

Many Americans were still unaware of the critical part played by these aircraft in the early hours of Operation Desert Storm. The advanced helicopters led the main strike forces into Bagdad, flying in advance of the first strike groups. Their mission was to take out surface-to-air missile sites and confuse the Iraqi radar defense with their electronic warfare systems.

Now six of those same helicopters flew low over the water toward the Egyptian coastline. The flight of helicopters altered their course slightly at twenty miles out, setting a final heading for the airport at Alexandria. Once feet dry over the shoreline, the helicopters anticipated a short transit of approximately one minute to the target site.

Upon arrival, pre-designated aircraft would land and deliver the Ranger force while other handpicked PAVLOWs popped up to five hundred feet. These aircraft would also establish a tight orbit around the airport ready to attack enemy reinforcements approaching the target or provide direct fire support for the Rangers.

The Rangers were heavily equipped, each man carrying upwards of ninety-five pounds of bullets, guns, rockets, claymore mines, and communication equipment. Unlike their SEAL brothers, the Rangers were designed to perform as shock troops, seize a target and then, if required, take the brunt of any enemy counter attack. They would typically hold on until relieved by a larger conventional force equipped with light mechanized capability, tanks, and dedicated air support.

In virtually every conflict since Vietnam the Rangers, Eighty-Second Airborne, Green Berets, and SEALs were employed on the ground well in advance of all other conventional forces. In Grenada the Rangers jumped in from five hundred feet to seize a key Cuban controlled airfield. In Panama, during Operation Just Cause, they jumped in to claim a critical airfield in a failed attempt to find the rouge leader Noriega in the early hours of the invasion.

Tonight's mission was a standard bread and butter situation and the Rangers were ready to lead the way. The Ranger officers and NCOs had planned the operation down to the very last detail. Every soldier knew his job. Every squad knew its assignment. The six helicopters would come in low, two or three feet over the airport tarmac. Once on the ground the Rangers would spread out into a patrol formation resembling the letter V.

The troop formations would advance across the target, moving to their assigned defensive positions. One group was responsible for seizing and controlling the critical airport entrance near the main road. Others would take over established east and west defense positions constructed and currently occupied by Egyptian military forces. The Rangers, like all special operations troops, expected intelligence estimates provided to them about the airport to be in error.

At the very least, the information would be inaccurate by the time they arrived. The intelligence types briefed the Rangers that only a few soldiers would be manning the defensive positions. They also said it was possible the airport would not be protected by regular Egyptian military forces. With the unrest going on throughout the country, it was highly likely most soldiers would have defected and returned to their homes to await the outcome. Of course, there wasn't a single Ranger who believed that would be the case.

Time and time again in their illustrious past the Rangers had been sent in against light opposition. More often than not, they found instead heavy mechanized troops, well dug in and occupied by motivated soldiers who didn't realize that the Americans were supposed to win easily.

Two nautical miles out, the aircrew commander, traveling in the lead helicopter, signaled the codeword AJAX. AJAX was phase line three, indicating that the force was now definitely in Egyptian territorial waters. This action was a violation of sovereign airspace and constituted an act of war by the United States. While it may seem meaningless to outside observers, America has always tried to restrain itself by limiting its military operations to allow the state department additional time to work its magic. However, tonight, having passed AJAX, the Rangers and the United States were fully committed.

The helicopters ripped through the night sky, spreading the formation slightly to make it more difficult for them to be hit by a single antiaircraft weapon. At one mile outbound the codeword ARROW was sent. From here the aircraft had thirty seconds before crossing the land-sea barrier. The PAVLOWs now broke into two formations and dropped to fifteen feet over the water. All their active sensors were up and operating at one hundred per cent, searching the coastline for active enemy coastal defense radars.

The radar systems were usually "slaved" to antiaircraft missile batteries to coordinate defense against enemy air attack of the Egyptian homeland. CHARLESTON, CHARLESTON, CHARLESTON! The feet dry code word was received by all six aircraft and passed on to their desert camouflaged warriors by the aircrew. In each helicopter NCOs were passing the sixty-second standby alert to each soldier. Most of the

Rangers had been ready to start fighting since leaving the NATO air base back in Italy. A few checked themselves one more time just to make their sergeant happy. Operation Sparrow Hawk was shifting into high gear!

Washington, D.C.

In the Pentagon crisis room, the duty officer watched as each of the code words flashed up on the screen. He was aware that once the Rangers were in place and the airport secured, the rest of the invasion would continue on a larger scale. The airhead established in Alexandria by the Rangers would allow continuing heavy forces to come in and land. The heavier mobile forces would then spread out and seize vital strategic targets in Alexandria.

The large open field adjacent to the airport could also be used as a drop zone, allowing the Eighty Second Airborne to insert and add to the growing troop presence on the ground. Within hours the United States would have seven thousand infantry troops on the ground with mechanized support, mobile artillery and a land based, forward operating site, at the airport. Tactical air assets could also use the Alexandria airfield as a logistics staging area for follow-on support operations probing further south toward Cairo.

The phone in the crisis situation room rang loudly, startling the duty officer. "Yes sir, this is Major Johnson!"

"Hello major, this is General Fitzpatrick. I'm calling for the chairman. What's the latest status report on Operation Sparrow Hawk?"

The duty officer's eyes scanned the brightly lit status board.

"Sir, the last codeword flashed was CHARLESTON. That means feet dry for the Rangers insertion aircraft. They should be within sight of the airfield at Alexandria right about now. And sir, the next codeword is

DOGMA. Receipt of DOGMA means the Rangers have secured the airfield."

The major paused, waiting for the senior officer on the other end of the line to acknowledge his report. The general asked only one question. "So as far as you know everything is going as planned for the SEALs?"

The duty officer replied immediately. "Well, general, I can assure you the code words from all pre-invasion operations have been received on schedule, including the SEALs at the airport. Sir, I suggest you give us a call back in about ten minutes. By then we should have hard information from all the operations currently underway."

The general mumbled a brief reply and hung up. After the call was completed, the major spotted the red light on another one of the phones as it started flashing. It was a silent phone and gave him a direct link to the commander Sixth Fleet in the Mediterranean. The duty officer picked up the phone, listened for a moment, and slowly put the receiver down. The caller had relayed a terrible message. Naval surveillance aircraft monitoring the Egyptian coastline had devastating news for the planners of Sparrow Hawk.

CHAPTER TWELVE

The Airport At Alexandria

The Egyptian commander of the air defense unit slowly lowered the binoculars, watching as the last American helicopter drifted like a falling leaf into the sea. The explosions had sent shock waves rippling across the sand dunes. The men of the missile battery nearest him were cheering.

The ambush had been a gamble. Employing an old trick out of an outdated Soviet training manual, the young air defense officer had decided to concentrate all his surface-to air missiles in a tight checkerboard pattern adjacent to the coastline. Then he placed visual spotters along the beach with hand-held radios to let him know exactly when the American air assault force was crossing the beach.

Since the Americans relied exclusively on radar to detect fire control radar emissions, they had no idea the air defenses were in their direct path. The concealed Egyptians needed only to be patient, firing their missiles into the Americans at point blank range. The officer knew their success had been a lucky break. He also knew the Americans wouldn't quit, and they wouldn't make the same mistake twice.

Headquarters–Commander, Sixth Fleet

Admiral Carden sat staring at the situation report passed to him by the Navy E2-C Hawkeye reconnaissance aircraft stationed off the coast of Egypt. On the wall nearby, a large operations status board displayed the exact position of every fleet asset in and around Egypt. It also showed the position of other allied and U.S. forces based in Italy and Spain, staged to support Operation Sparrow Hawk.

Shuffling the folders in front of him, Admiral Carden continued to consume a consolidated intelligence summary describing how the entire Ranger strike force had been eliminated by a highly concentrated battery of Egyptian surface-to-air missiles. It appeared that advance knowledge of American military intentions was forwarded to the Egyptians from somewhere in Europe.

The national security agency was reviewing its signals surveillance records to pinpoint the exact phone call. Once traced, other steps would be taken to ensure it did not happen again. A footnote in the report suggested the Egyptians might have employed an old Soviet air defense tactic effective in other areas of conflict in times past.

The admiral leaned back, rocking gently. During the Vietnam War he and his squadron flew iron hand SAM suppression missions off the U.S.S Ranger to clear the way for naval air strikes into the North. These iron hand missions were tasked with lighting up the enemy search radar linked to the Russian surface-to-air missile, or SAM, sites. Once the fire control radars kicked in to shoot down the iron hand flight, the pilots onboard the navy A-6 intruder aircraft would fire off their radar seeking missiles. The SAM sites would be eliminated, thus clearing the way for the main strike force.

The trick worked for a while. Then the boys in Hanoi came up their own sweet little trick. They clustered their SAMs together and fired them all at once, relying on a sophisticated system of coastal spotters stretching inland to Hanoi. The SAMs would let the iron hand mission fly by and wait for a larger flight indicating a main effort by the Americans. The SAMs would execute a snap shot when the Americans were in view, lighting up their fire control radars and firing the missiles virtually at the same time.

The men flying those air force PAVLOWs were too young to remember such hard learned lessons. To them Vietnam was ancient history. However, somebody in the Egyptian military was clearly aware enough to use those same lessons against the Americans now. Admiral Carden pondered the dilemma facing him. Without Rangers holding the airport, the follow-on phase two forces wouldn't be able to utilize a friendly defended location to facilitate executing the invasion.

That meant the airport at Alexandria would still have to be captured and held one way or another to ensure the success of Operation Sparrow Hawk. The Chief of Staff stood by patiently watching the admiral commanding the U.S. Sixth Fleet. He cleared his throat, trying to gain the admiral's attention. Admiral Carden looked up.

"Yes?"

"Well sir," the Chief of Staff began, "I was thinking. You know, we do have forces in close proximity to that airport. The SEALs are due to check in within the next ten minutes. Even allowing for a little bit of slop in their schedule, their reconnaissance team should be on that target very soon. There just might be a chance these guys can take out the limited guard force and control the airport long enough for us to get some marines on the ground."

The admiral squinted.

"How many SEALs do we have on the ground at the airport, commander?"

"Sir, uh, eight I believe," replied the now nervous staff officer.

"Eight SEALs?" The admiral asked.

"Yes sir," according to intelligence estimates this airport is very lightly patrolled and most of the troops likely to be stationed around the airfield are poorly trained draftees. Our boys believe that the Egyptians most likely course of action would be to evacuate the area at the first sign of trouble."

Admiral Carden looked up to check out the status board. Two minutes passed. His Chief of Staff shifted his weight uneasily from foot to foot. The admiral finally broke the silence. "Draft an immediate message to the Chief of Naval Operations, and forward a copy to the Pentagon. Tell them my recommendation is to employ the SEAL reconnaissance team currently in place at the Alexandria airport, to act as pathfinders for another assault group. And Frank, when the SEALs call in, tell them to take up positions without drawing too much attention to themselves. Let them know we plan to send in another group, ASAP!"

"Now Frank, I also want your operations guys to get hopping on a new action plan for a second assault group. I want the draft in my hands in thirty minutes. Consider use of any and all forces not already committed to other missions. Also, have our tactics and operations people put together a suppression mission to take out those damn SAMs!"

"Yes sir! I'll get on it immediately."

Frank turned on his heel, barely concealing his relief that things were moving forward at last.

One Mile From The Airport At Alexandria

Matt hustled to catch up with Boone grabbed him by the shoulder strap and gently directed the point man off to the side of the road. The entire team was out of breath. Boone had pushed them pretty hard, covering more ground than Matt would have thought possible since executing the hasty ambush. However, it was time to play it smart. Speed was not as important as stealth now that they were within sight of the target. Matt whispered.

"We don't want to get stupid here, Boone. Let's slow it down and spread out. The airport is only a couple of meters away from here."

Boone didn't respond. He didn't have to say anything. He only nodded in acknowledgment of Matt's command. Matt turned around and whispered his instructions to Jorgy, who turned and passed the word on down the line. Soon the entire team knew what was going on. Moving off the side of the road even further, Boone picked a target entry point approximately one hundred yards to the right of the roadway.

The SEALs could barely see each other as they followed Boone through the low brush. Matt glanced back and made a chopping motion with his hand. Moving his hand left, and then right several times. Jorgy repeated the signal. Upon receiving the signal, each man would step to his field of fire.

Since the SEALs had alternating fields of fire, their movements effectively split their patrol file into two staggered columns. They also doubled the distance between them. Although they were spread out, it made the frogmen a more difficult target to ambush.

The SEALs could hear firing and explosions far away in the city. Matt wasn't sure if that had anything to do with the American operation, or if the locals were only blowing off steam. Matt guessed it wasn't the American attack. Not yet. Matt knew that when the Americans began their action, all hell would really break loose. First the gunships would move into their fire support orbits and start to pound critical targets. Air strikes and the helicopter gun ships would execute strafing runs attempting to isolate and eliminate the Egyptian air and ground units before they could deploy. One thing was certain, Matt thought, it was going to be one hell of a show.

The SEALs patrolled another four minutes before Boone signaled to the others to form a defensive perimeter. Matt could just about see the outline of the airport's control tower from where they stopped and that was close enough for now. He knew he had to make a communications call very soon. But what Matt really wanted to do was send Boone and Oby up ahead to conduct a reconnaissance of the target area first.

The intelligence boys had assured the SEALs during pre-mission briefings that the target should be soft. This meant little to no formal military presence on-site, and most likely nobody but looters looking for a few discounts during the social chaos. Matt was hoping that was the case, but the chances were just as good that the spooks were wrong, and that meant his platoon might find themselves up to their asses in alligators. If that happened he would be unable to stop and communicate anything to anybody.

Matt made his decision. He sent Boone and Oby off for a quick look at the target, and then directed Wells to send the on target codeword.

Headquarters–Commander, Sixth Fleet

The Sixth Fleet commander looked up as his Chief of Staff walked back into the situation room. "Sir, we have our reply from Washington."

"Yes?" said the admiral. "What did they say?"

The Chief of Staff answered. "I'm sorry sir, uh yes, they said yes. Yes to everything, sir, yes to your whole concept. They said there's no time to argue with your proposed solution. And they don't have a plan in hand to try anything else. Washington also directed you to modify the SEALs original mission statement. You are cleared to communicate the new tasking when they make their next communications call."

Admiral Carden looked down for a moment. To expect eight lightly armed SEALs to occupy and control an airport was unrealistic. The tasking had to be communicated in such a way as to give the young officer in command a clear idea of what was expected of him. The new tasking should direct the small force to prevent re-enforcement of the target by the Egyptians. It should also tell them to do their best to help support the arrival of the second assault force.

The admiral jotted down the essence of a coherent mission order for the SEALs. The Chief of Staff had something else to share.

"Sir, one more thing. They basically put it in your hands. They implied that if this operation fails, you will be left holding the bag and maybe worse, if it goes right, somebody inside the D.C. beltway is probably going to take credit for your idea."

Admiral Carden looked up and sighed.

"Frank, those poor bastards on the ground are about to be told to seize an airport because a much larger Ranger force couldn't get there to do the job! Instead of worrying about credit and blame, let's focus on putting the show together!"

"Ah, yes sir," the Chief of Staff mumbled sheepishly.

The admiral continued. "Tell our communications people to pass on the new orders as soon as they make contact with the SEALs. I don't want any screw-ups, Frank. No misunderstandings. They need to know they must stay there and support the landing of the second group!"

"Yes sir, I'll make absolutely sure it's clear." With that said, the Chief of Staff turned and departed in a hurry.

Airport At Alexandria

Matt was getting impatient. Wells seemed to be taking forever with the radio equipment. Matt decided to use the delay to check everybody's readiness. He spoke to the platoon in a hushed whisper. "Make sure all of you have your shit together. We have no idea who might be waiting for us on this target and I want everybody paying particular attention to their assigned fields of fire. We are going to ease in there, look around, move forward, and look around some more. Anticipate contact, every step of the way. Is that clear?"

The enlisted SEALs nodded quietly.

"Go ahead and check your gear as a buddy pair. One man on watch, while his buddy goes over his equipment, then switch." The speech finished, Matt hissed at Wells. "Are you finished with that stupid SATCOM radio yet? We need to start making tracks!"

The target codeword had to be sent via satellite this time, rather than relayed through the airborne communications link on secure UHF. Wells leaned closer to Matt.

"Hey LT, I've finished passing the codeword but they said they have new traffic. Could you help me out here, boss? I need you to jot down the message as I say it."

Matt pulled out his green patrol log and nodded in readiness. The handset crackled to life.

"X-ray seven, I have a new mission tasking for you. I say again new mission tasking! Are you ready to copy? Over."

Wells' eyes locked with Matt's. "Sir, they said there's a new mission."

Matt calmly studied his radioman, trying to appear unaffected by the comment. Whatever this was, it probably wasn't going to be good. "Go ahead and take the message."

"Yes sir," Wells replied, pressing the transmission button on his SATCOM radio. "This is X-ray seven, go ahead with your traffic."

"X-ray seven, this is whiskey-niner bravo. New mission tasking, seize and hold your objective. I say again, seize and hold your objective. Primary strike force has aborted. New strike force will be at your position before dawn. You will provide security support for their insertion, how copy over?"

Wells repeated the message back. Matt still hadn't moved his pencil. Matt still couldn't believe what he'd heard. Seize and hold the entire airport? There was no way eight men could seize and hold an entire airport. What the hell had happened to the Rangers? Where the hell were those guys? Matt could feel his anger and resentment getting the best of him. He had to regain control. The others were watching him.

"Wells, call them back. Ask them if there are any new signals or code words for our link up with the new assault force or do we use the linkup package for the original force."

"Yes sir."

Wells answered, calming a little after hearing Matt's tone.

"Whiskey-niner bravo this is X-ray seven, please confirm that assault force linkup procedures remain the same, over."

The answer came immediately.

"X-ray seven this is whiskey-niner bravo, roger your last. We have no further traffic. Anything for us, over?"

Wells looked at Matt but Matt just shook his head. Wells completed the call. "That's a negative whiskey-niner bravo, Xray seven out!"

There was a stunned silence throughout the perimeter. Jorgy was the first to speak.

"Shit, boss! There must be some kinda mistake!"

Doc chimed in. "What gives, LT? Can they do that? Can they just tell us to attack an airport with eight guys? What dumb ass desk jockey came up with this bone head idea?"

"You know it wasn't anyone from the teams," Cruise injected. "One of our guys wouldn't let this happen!"

"You got that right," Wells mumbled.

Chief Auger eased into the center of the perimeter so he could get face-to-face with Matt. The chief asked the question on everyone's mind, though they already knew the answer.

"Hey boss, do we really have to do this? I mean, can't we tell them, no? Maybe someone screwed up and they don't know there are only eight of us out here! There's got to be some way we can reconfirm this! Damn it, sir, we're SEALs not storm troopers!"

Matt stared at a small spot on the ground near his worn boot tip for a few seconds before replying.

"Chief, we've got our orders and those orders are we have a new mission. They didn't tell us how to do it; they just said we had to do it. So let's go up and take a look at this place and think things through."

Matt addressed the stunned men around him. "We have a lot of fire power here, guys, plenty of food and water and our training to rely on. Every one of you knows his craft."

Looking back at the chief, Matt spoke firmly. "Chief, let's just go up and take a look."

The chief looked from side to side to see if any of the men were buying this. All he saw were men doing their job, watching the area around their perimeter. Looking back at Matt he realized they were committed to this insanity. He smiled halfheartedly and then sighed. "Okay boss, whatever you say."

Matt placed his hand on the chief's shoulder. "Hoo-ya, chief! Remember back in BUD/S training? If you can feel the pain, you know you're still alive. Now while this may be painful, I intend to get through it with everyone in one piece! Come on, let's make it happen!"

Chief Auger turned and passed the word. "Okay, you all heard what the LT said, let's saddle up!"

Boone and Oby were returning from their scouting patrol. Matt took them aside to hear their report and to let them in on the mission change. Neither of the men even blinked at hearing the news. Again, Matt wondered where such men came from. The Navy had selected and trained the very best America had to offer and placed them in his care. Matt had to measure up and earn the right to lead them.

"All right Boone, take us in."

The SEALs stood up and formed into a staggered file formation once again. Boone cautiously walked toward the security fence surrounding the airport. He led the patrol to the left and then back to the right every fifteen yards, zig-zagging to the target.

By moving this way Boone could view the target entry point at various angles. If anybody did spot them, they would have a tough time determining how many SEALs were approaching. Because they were spread out in a staggered column, the SEALs hoped the Egyptian observation positions along this side of the target would be fooled believing there were far more American troops in the woods heading in their direction then there were. Hopefully this mis-information would delay any counter attack until the Egyptians felt they were sufficiently reinforced. By then, the SEALs would already be in position.

It took about six or seven minutes for the SEALs to arrive at the edge of the airfield. It was now very easy to see the five-foot high chain link fence encircling the target. The mesh pattern stood out clearly against the glow of Alexandria's city lights. Looking through his night vision scope Matt could see that the immediate area was clear of enemy personnel. But his view of the rest of the airfield was partially blocked by metal aircraft hangars.

The structures were flimsy, consisting of corrugated tin sides and fiberglass roofing. Here and there, along the line of hangars, Matt could make out larger commercial buildings that probably held more significant aircraft. Far down the runway and to his right, he could just make out the control tower. A small, unimposing building, constructed of simple cinder blocks.

According to their intelligence briefing, the airport could operate at night due to the presence of a radar-activated beacon at the end of the runway. The beacon was electronically activated by an aircraft on final approach and once activated the runway lit up like a Christmas tree. This meant the airport did not require the control tower to be manned at night. The conclusion of the intelligence types was there were few if any airport personnel on duty.

However, considering the recent escalating hostilities, Matt felt in his gut that such a strategic location could not possibly go unguarded or unmanned. His night vision scope didn't indicate the presence of any lights in the vicinity of the control tower. His decision made, Matt turned back to Cruise and pointed to the fence.

"Do it!" Matt ordered.

Cruise nodded. He leaned forward and began to cut an entryway through the chain link fence with his wire cutters while the rest of the team formed a horseshoe shaped security perimeter. Cruise was able to cut a man-sized hole in the fence in about two minutes. Boone was first to slip through, moving away from the fence to allow room for the rest of his team to assemble. Next came Jorgy with his M-60, setting security in the direction of the control tower. Matt then slipped through and turned to help the others clear the fence line.

Once the team was inside the target area Matt directed Boone to take the platoon to the closest corrugated steel building near the runway. The runway was approximately fourteen hundred yards long at its narrowest point, closer to the ocean; it was only one hundred yards wide.

As it stretched inland, it grew wider until it was finally three hundred yards wide near the control tower. The majority of military aircraft and a few of the smaller personal jets belonging to affluent Egyptians were staged up near the wider southern end of the airport. The various aircraft were staged both in hangars and outside on concrete aprons. The aprons were connected with small taxiways leading out to the main runways.

A small jet trying to leave the airport would only require a few minutes to power up, turn onto the runway, and get airborne. If Matt was going to hold the airport for the next assault group, he would have to find a way to keep aircraft from departing. But that wasn't really his biggest problem. His biggest problem was knowing what to do if the target became infested with enemy troops prior to the assault force's insertion.

CHAPTER THIRTEEN

Matt gave the signal to circle up in a perimeter next to the first hangar. A dim light bulb above the double door cast just enough light on the ground for Matt to explain his plan of action. He crouched in the dirt and sketched the outline of the airport.

"Chief, come on over here for a second."

Chief Auger detached himself from the circle and moved closer, looking down at the shapes Matt had made on the ground. He watched as Matt's finger added to the general outline of the runway, making large squares to depict some of the commercial hangars at the southern end. Matt made an X on the southeastern point of the runway where the control tower was located.

"Okay, chief, here's how I see it. We have eight guys with only enough firepower to fight for a short period of time. So it's obvious we can't get into any long drawn out firefights or the game will be over. I think we need to find a good observation position on the edge of the runway with our backs to an exit. Maybe cut a hole in the fence so we can get everyone though fast; that is, if we have to make a run for it."

The chief was in agreement. "Sure, I see what you're getting at, sir. We can set up some basic security and get as much standoff weaponry in position as possible. I'm thinking the M-203's and rifles can handle basic area control and fire suppression. We can set up Oby with his fifty-caliber to deal with any armored vehicles that enter the area or any aircraft that try to take off. Do you think we should use Jorgy's heavy gun up front or hold it in reserve?"

"You've read my mind, chief. I'd like to hold off using the M-60 for any kind of basic reaction to movement on the airfield because we may need that if and when were counterattacked by heavier forces. If we stay loose, keep good security and pop anything that moves, we can give the Rangers coming in a fighting chance. What do you think?"

Chief Auger thought the plan over one more time. It wasn't half bad. It was basic, easy to explain to the guys, it didn't require spreading out all over the target, and best of all it didn't require moving out into the open. If things got too hairy, they could just back up, move through the hole in the fence, and get the hell out of Dodge. Yeah, the chief liked the plan.

"Not bad, boss, not bad at all. But I tell you what—I wouldn't pass this plan along to the higher ups. They're probably sweating bullets right now wondering how the hell you're going to pull this off. They are going to try to micro-manage this deal and you know it! Give them too much slack and they will have us charging the damn control tower!"

Matt nodded in agreement. "Got you, chief. If they ask, we'll just tell them that we are still moving into in position. And if things really get out of control, we'll send the abort code word and get off the target. There's a chance we could still be of some assistance to the assault force with Oby's fifty-caliber if he can find a place to fire from outside the airport."

Chief Auger nodded, basic SEAL tactics. KISS—keep it simple and stupid. The guys will appreciate this, the chief thought. The chief went around the circle briefing each of the SEALs. Matt moved up to Boone and picked out a hangar approximately half way up the airfield. Boone figured the distance at fifty or sixty meters.

"LT, I think we should stay behind the hangars the whole way there. We can move in the shadows and heavy underbrush between the chain link fence and the corrugated steel structures. That would limit our exposure and maybe give us a chance to get in position without being detected."

Matt agreed with the assessment. "Good call, Boone. The chief 's almost finished briefing the others. As soon as he's done, we'll get rolling."

A few seconds later the chief walked up to Matt and gave him a thumbs-up.

"All right," Matt said just loud enough for everyone to hear. "Let's do this thing!"

The SEALs stood up in an orderly fashion and followed Boone. The point man wove in and around the garbage strewn in the gap between the back of the hangars and the chain link fence. The shadows cast by the lights in the front of the hangars created an eerie atmosphere. Each SEAL stepped carefully, fearful of creating any noise as they made their final approach. It took approximately ten minutes for the SEALs to patrol to the pre-selected hangar.

The large commercial hangar was empty. The two sliding doors were pushed back to leave the building open and accessible. Boone walked into the structure with his rifle at the ready. Since it was apparent the hangar was clear of enemy threats Boone waved Matt forward to join him. The two SEALs took a look around their new home.

"You know, Boone. By setting up in the back of the hangar we could reduce our exposure to direct fire and limit the enemy's view of our team's position."

"I think you're right, boss. No sense letting them know how many of us there are."

Boone agreed. In the back of the hangar there was an unlocked door. Matt indicated to the chief that he wanted it propped open.

"Cruise!" Matt called. "Go back to the chain link fence and cut a hole large enough for two or three people to get through. Take Doc with you. Keep an eye on our rear back there while you are at it."

Cruise nodded and motioned for Doc to join him. The two enlisted men walked through the open back door and left the hangar. Matt placed Jorgy in the southern corner of the hangar so he could stay out of site, keeping his machine gun out of the action until really needed. The chief and Wells setup in the northern corner so they had a clear field of fire toward the most likely route of approach, the main feeder road coming into the tower to the south.

Matt decided to pair up with his machine gunner, in the end, their respective positions creating a deadly crisscrossing of each SEALs field of fire. Matt still intended to remain hidden until it was absolutely necessary. Oby was allowed to choose his own firing position for proper employment of his sniper rifle. He eventually selected an eight-foot tall industrial trash container sitting next to the hangar.

The dumpster was on the southern side, allowing Oby a clear view of the entrance to the airport. Oby climbed to the top of the large steel box and reached down to accept his gear and weapon from Boone. Boone crawled up next. Boone's job was to provide personal security for the sniper while he worked. Boone would also assist Oby with spotting targets and reloading the big fifty-caliber rifle.

Back inside the hangar, Matt called up Cruise and directed that he and Doc remain near the fence to observe the route north and south behind the buildings on their side of the airport. They were responsible for using their night vision equipment and their ears to give early warning if anybody tried to sneak up on the back door.

Matt took a slow look around the hangar. A two-man rear security element, a two man sniper element, Jorgy in reserve, and three riflemen with crisscrossing fields of fire. Yeah, Matt thought, guess this is about the best we can do. Matt had relieved Wells of the secure UHF handheld radio so he could participate fully in any fighting should they be forced to engage the Egyptians.

Matt checked his watch. Dawn was rushing toward them. If the Rangers didn't arrive before sunrise Matt's platoon would be easy to find and attack. Right now the night was his only support. The airborne communications relay should be on station by now. Matt decided to try the UHF radio to pass the next code word. The next signal was HOME-STEAD. This conveyed the SEALs were on target and in position.

Matt made contact on the first try. The strength of the signal meant the aircraft was very close, possibly just a mile or two off the coast. There wasn't a message for Matt and that was a very good sign. He still expected the higher ups to interfere and micro-manage the event on the ground. It might still happen as the big boys eventually start sweating out their decision to put eight men in harms way on a virtual suicide mission. What a dumb shit drill this is, Matt thought. It's just as well they left him alone. Matt wasn't in the mood to be diplomatic.

Office Of The Commander–Sixth Fleet

Frank was pleased with his work. The final arrangements for the strike package were almost in place. Aircraft from the Teddy Roosevelt battle group were tasked to swoop in low over the water, directed and supported by a host of specialty units. A combination of air force AWACs aircraft, and airborne command and control or "A,B triple C" aircraft, were assigned to monitor the entire operation. Add to that a flight of ground attack F-15 Eagles in standby.

These battle-tested airframes were capable of multiple strike sorties at night and in all weather conditions. All together fifteen strike air-craft supported by twenty-one support planes. The entire strike pack-age was fed by KC-130 air-to-air refuel tankers and controlled by the Teddy Roosevelt battle group commander. The sophisticated aircraft and navy ships deployed in the eastern Mediterranean since the very start of Operation Sparrow Hawk had shared the collected radar emissions from the earlier Ranger insertion mission.

The mix of signals had been painstakingly organized and deciphered by American experts. The Egyptian radar and communications transmissions were identified and their sources pinpointed. Using this information, especially the presence of small unit radio activity near the ambush site, American F-15's would take out the area where the Egyptian SAMs were operating. One of the key weapons being used by the strike force was a clever concept referred to as cluster munitions. These bombs dispersed thousands of smaller bomblets from an altitude of five hundred feet over the selected target.

The bomblets completely covered an area half the size of a football field. Upon contact with the ground the explosives detonated, spraying a deadly pattern of shrapnel with devastating effect. After the initial strikes, other high explosive cluster munitions would be dropped in a checkerboard pattern around the area. The purpose of the HE bomblets was to destroy material and disable equipment. Once the SAM site was defeated, a signal would be sent releasing the second Ranger assault force from a control point off the coast.

Just prior to the SAM suppression strike, the "A,B triple C" boys would advance the Rangers incrementally by phase lines, closer and closer to the Egyptian land mass. The idea was to coordinate the SAM strike with the Ranger insertion with a minimum loss of time. Everyone involved was aware time was critical to the survival of eight Americans on target.

The second assault force was a beefed-up version of the first one. A flight of CH-47 helicopters containing soldiers from the eighty-second airborne would follow PAVLOWs carrying the Rangers. The Ranger's mission was to deploy throughout the airport and secure the facility.

Army air traffic control personnel would also accompany the Rangers. They were critical to getting the airport up and running to support the main U.S. invasion effort. Once the Rangers were in control, the airborne troops would land and set up heavier defensive positions. The paratroopers would also push the perimeter out beyond the airport boundaries to control the major choke points and roadways.

Then the last phase would begin with sorties of C-130 Hercules cargo aircraft, flying in, depositing hundreds more airborne infantry, and heavier transport to include the Bradley fighting vehicle. If all went well, within thirty minutes a total of eight hundred elite American troops would be on the ground controlling the airport. The continuous flow of large-scale forces could then begin in earnest. The chief of staff picked up the new strike plan and left his office bound for the situation room. The admiral will be very happy he thought, and I won't be in the doghouse anymore!

CHAPTER FOURTEEN

Banadar's Headquarters

Banadar sat quietly reading the Koran. He believed in the old ways, the desert ways. A true Muslim should devote time to the study of Allah. In modern Egypt, people did as little as possible by way of observance. In Banadar's opinion they had lost touch with the Prophet and his teachings.

In his new Egypt things would be different. Banadar's solitude was shattered abruptly. The door flew open with a bang!

"Enlightened one!" a disheveled soldier shouted. "The infidels are here!"

Banadar calmly peered at the frenzied man. "Stop your babbling and tell me what you know to be true."

The man lowered his head. "I will try, Enlightened One."

He took a moment to regain control. "Sir, the word arrived just minutes ago that one of our roving military patrols was wiped out near the Alexandria airport. And sir, only a few minutes later one of our missile defense batteries near the coastline reported shooting down several American helicopters. It's believed by our air force that these aircraft were traveling toward the airport!"

The messenger breathlessly completed his report, lowering his eyes to avoid Banadar's stare. Banadar closed the holy book and stood up. He walked casually over to the large map of northern Egypt displayed prominently on the opposite wall. The Alexandria airport was not an obvious military target. Why would the Americans waste their time there of all places? Banadar looked toward the south on the map. Cairo should be their focal point. Not Alexandria.

Just then another soldier barged into the room. Banadar did not look at the man as he repeated the same report submitted by the first messenger. He raised his hand gently and the man stopped in mid-sentence.

Banadar continued to ponder the situation. There was something here he couldn't see. Something that his intuition told him was very important. The ambushed Egyptian patrol had been very large. Banadar estimated that it would have taken at least twenty to thirty enemy troops to eliminate a patrol of that size. But an even more important question was, why would an enemy force of that size, be on that particular road?

Could the Americans be trying to cut off access to the airport? Or for that matter, were they part of a much larger strike force that somehow had penetrated Egyptian territory without being detected? And if so, was their objective seizing the airport?

Banadar's eyes roamed over the map focusing his attention on the area in and around the city of Alexandria. He needed to understand why the airport's position would be of any importance to the Americans.

His eyes eventually moved back to the dark black line representing the airport on the map. Helicopters just offshore? Banadar froze suddenly. Alexandria has a port! The Americans needed the port of Alexandria for their amphibious ships! Now it all fell into place. The airport would serve as a critical base for American re-supply and support of the debarkation of marines in the port of Alexandria. It would also provide the Americans a launching point for extended action inland. The American strategy would also cut off the supply of food and essential materials to Cairo.

Without the flow of foreign commerce through Alexandria's harbor and airport, Cairo would become a big city full of hungry people in a very short time. Banadar stepped back from the map. The airport was the key! If he could thwart the American plan to establish a foothold there, he might buy enough time to move his air forces closer to the coast. Right now the Egyptian fighters were dispersed inland to avoid U.S. pre-emptive strikes from the carrier battle group offshore.

If he was successful defending the airport, the Americans could still try to use helicopters elsewhere. However, Banadar knew the enemy's helicopters were much too small to bring in enough troops to really count for much. Denying the airport would set back the American time table, giving his recently enlightened high command enough breathing room to mount a vigorous defense. The key was still the airport!

Banadar turned and brushed past the two messengers standing by the door. He barked out orders as he cleared the doorway.

"Have my personal vehicle ready for immediate departure!" Banadar twisted back around to speak to his personal aide. "Make sure there's a lorry with at least twenty troops ready to accompany me to the airport. We leave in ten minutes! Radio ahead to the airport and place them on alert. Inform them I will be arriving within the hour!"

As he left the building, Banadar bent down and picked up his AK-47 automatic rifle from beside the door. Slinging it across his back, he walked to his jeep feeling confident Allah was showing him the way to victory against the Americans.

The Airport–Alexandria

Matt studied the layout from the platoon's new firing position. He could see only limited troop activity in and around the main tower area but did spot at least one, two-man roving patrol on the opposite side of the runway near the commercial hangars. Matt was sure no one had spotted them yet.

Even though the airport was well lit, it was still difficult to see any detail between and behind the line of buildings. And while the SEALs night vision equipment was useful to a point, out beyond seventy-five yards, the high tech equipment didn't reveal much more than the naked eye.

Time passed without incident. Every so often Matt could see movement in some of the buildings that had office spaces attached. Looking at his watch, Matt realized that very soon they would be running into daylight. Maybe they would luck out and make it to dawn without a fight. Matt walked over to Chief Auger.

"Well, chief, are we lucky or what? It looks like the heavyweights might get here without any fireworks."

The chief waited politely for Matt to finish. "LT, we just chopped up a bunch of their guys back there on the road. Do you remember that? My guess is the Egyptians have put two and two together by now. Maybe we will get lucky as you say, but I don't believe in miracles, sir. As far as I'm concerned, whatever the big boys at Sixth Fleet are planning to do, they better do it quick!"

Matt didn't want to argue with his chief at a time like this. But he still thought things were looking up.

"All right, chief, we'll keep our powder dry. I just checked with Oby and Wells and things are still normal. I really don't plan to start a fight if I can help it." Matt's earpiece squeaked to life in his ear.

"Hey boss, this is Oby." Matt realized he might have spoken too soon.

"I've got a small column of light vehicles moving along the road near the entrance to the airfield. It's hard to tell but there may be as many as three or four of them. Some are carrying troops and one may be a command jeep. Okay, wait just a sec, now they're slowing down and pulling into the parking lot behind the control tower!"

Oby twisted slightly, bringing his fifty-caliber sniper rifle around and into position. He set his sub-machine gun aside. That peashooter was retired for now. His position atop the dumpster wasn't the greatest firing position, but at least the bad guys would have to come out into the open to take a good shot at him.

"Boss, there are about twenty or thirty guys piling out of the trucks and I don't think they are air traffic controllers!"

Matt listened to his sniper's report, a grim look on his face.

"Understood Oby. Just keep an eye on things and let me know if anything changes. LT out."

Matt could hear the sound of more military vehicles now coming down the road near the northern end of the runway. He strained to see if he could detect headlights or any movement on the road but the trees and brush along the elevated side of the northern part of the runway blocked his view. Chief Auger addressed Matt from the hangar shadows.

"Hey boss, sounds like we are about to have company."

"That's right, chief," Matt replied. "Oby reported several trucks just pulled into the tower parking lot and started deploying troops. I just heard what sounded like more showing up. Oby's going to give us a heads up as soon as he spots them aggressively moving into the target area."

"Well, whatever happens, we can only do—what we can do, and if it ain't enough, we need to get the hell out of Dodge! Right LT?"

Matt looked at his assistant platoon commander and smiled.

"Don't worry, chief, I don't believe in being a hero!"

No heroes here, Matt thought. Isn't that ironic! The whole reason he became a SEAL was to try to become a hero. The thought of his father earning glory in combat, going through the same experience he was now facing, hadn't entered Matt's mind until now. In a strange way Matt felt a new sort of kinship with his father. Arthur Barrett had led men in combat. But one distinction was worth noting. While the old man walked away wearing the big blue, many of the men under his command didn't walk away at all.

Matt was a smarter, wiser person now than when he was a teenager, admiring a pretty medal in his father's den. Back then he had hoped someday to measure up. He realized now that being a hero was getting the job done right and bringing your men back alive. If Matt could do that, he would achieve something his father never could.

Out here it was just you and your men, no staffs, and no bullshit grading systems, nobody to second-guess your decisions. And if they didn't like the way you accomplished your mission, tough shit. The only opinions that really counted when it came right down to it, were those of the men who served with you on target. Yeah, the chief was right. We certainly don't want to be heroes. When you thought of heroes in the teams they were guys that were placed in bad situations, suicide missions that put frogmen in harms way for all the wrong reasons. Missions just like this one.

Control Tower–Alexandria Airport

Banadar walked away from his jeep with a purposeful stride.

"Where is the company commander?" he shouted. "I want him now!" The young officer scrambled to catch up with Banadar. He caught up just as his leader entered the tower facility. "Do not step all over me you fool! I want you to send out heavier patrols on both sides of the airport."

Banadar walked into the first floor office where he had been told a map of the airport layout could be found. "Here and here!" he said, stabbing a finger at the wall chart. "I want you to aggressively patrol behind the commercial hangars. Tell your men to follow the fence line and report anything out of the ordinary!"

The young company commander saluted and stepped away, afraid to ask any questions. Banadar called for access to a radio. He wanted to speak to the patrols already deployed around the airport. Banadar had already briefly contacted the infantry squad patrolling the airport while en route to the airport control tower. The sentries and roving patrols had reported they heard some shooting earlier in the night way off in the distance but so far no sign of the Americans.

Banadar was sure the men had heard the American ambush. He tried to raise the sentries once more. After a short discussion Banadar replaced the radio hand set. There was nothing to report. He didn't want to tell his men there was a possibility American forces could be attacking their location very soon. If his men knew too much, there was a chance they would lose heart and run. No, it was better to keep them in the dark for now.

Four of his personal bodyguards moved about with him as Banadar completed his inspection of the control tower area. Either the Americans or the British had trained most of the Egyptians at the airport during NATO exercises. Of course they never believed the skills that they were passing on to their Egyptian friends would be turned back on them.

Since the time of the peace accords between Egypt and Israel, Egypt had been treated like a puppet of the western governments. The American President Jimmy Carter bribed Anwar Sadat with billions in U.S. aid. All Sadat had to do was betray Islam. Since the late seventies Egypt had lain like a whore with the west. But now the arrogant west was about to find out how puppets fight!

The bodyguards remained with Banadar, watching him pace around the room. He needed time to think. He needed time to devise a nasty surprise for the American invasion force.

Hangar Position

Matt's earpiece crackled to life again. "Hey boss, it's Oby. It looks like there's a small group detaching from the tower. And they are moving to our side of the neighborhood. Oh shit, LT! They just slipped behind the hangars. If they patrol down the fence line, I estimate their ETA at our back door in four or five minutes. Did you get that, LT?"

Matt's mind was churning. Less than five minutes! Do we take out the patrol or do we try to evade them? Do we engage the patrol at a distance, or do we wait until they get in close and personal? Matt's thoughts were interrupted by Oby asking again if he had received the message.

"Yeah Oby, I got your message," Matt replied. "I'm working it. Just keep a look out to our front. Break! Wells, this is the LT. Did you copy Oby's traffic?"

"Roger that, LT!" replied Wells. "We have approximately eight to ten of these guys moving down the back fence line heading in our direction ETA four minutes. What's the call, boss?"

"You should spot them first, Wells," Matt said. "Keep your night vision goggles on and give us an indication when you see any movement. When you do spot them, I need your best guess ETA as soon as you can give it to me. If you don't think you can spot them from where you are sitting, move around back there until you have a better observation position."

"Roger, boss. We'll be in touch."

Wells turned to brief Doc on all the fun. Matt walked over to Chief Auger again. "Okay, chief, it looks like show time."

"What's up, boss?" the chief asked.

"Oby said he spotted eight to ten guys moving down the back fence line coming in behind the hangars. He figures three or four minutes before they are on top of us. I told Wells and Doc to keep an eye out and let us know when they see anybody moving back there. I really don't want to get into a fistfight but we can't move out of here now. There's only twenty minutes left before the Rangers arrive."

"Well, I think you are right about that, boss," Chief Auger said, nodding. "This isn't a real SEAL job anyway so we have to think about what we can actually accomplish here. Maybe we should radio the assault force and tell them and those headquarters types that we have about four minutes before we start engaging enemy forces and ask for their ETA. Then let's hit these goons walking the fence line as hard as we can! Ambushing this patrol reduces the number of bad guys on target, and it serves notice on everyone else out there who wants a piece of us! Once the cat's out of the bag we can just raise hell and kick ass until it's time to run! If we're lucky enough to stick around until the assault force gets here, even better!"

Matt saw the simplicity of the chief's logic and nodded in agreement. "Okay chief, you stay here and make the radio report on our status." Matt handed him the UHF radio.

He turned to the big machine gunner. "Jorgy! Lets go! I've finally got some work for that clump you carry around."

Jorgy jumped up and followed Matt through the door at the rear of the hangar. They joined Doc and Wells just as they were about to send the alert call. Matt and Jorgy didn't need any help seeing the Egyptian patrol. Wells was pointing right at the enemy formation. Matt took inventory of his firepower. He could get Oby off the dumpster to help engage the oncoming patrol but in all likelihood the reaction to the ambush would be from the tower area. Besides, there wasn't enough time now. It was better for Oby to stay in position to deal with any other patrols across the wide-open area of the runway and tower area.

Matt crawled over to Jorgy. Leaning down, he whispered in his ear. Jorgy nodded and moved up to Wells to pass the word along.

CHAPTER FIFTEEN

BOOM! The loud report of Oby's rifle shook the hangar. Matt knew Oby would've called him on the radio if he'd had time. Matt could now hear Boone's M-16 opening up also. Wells came over the radio.

"What the hell's going on?" Wells was shouting into the handset.

Matt rolled over next to Jorgy. "Don't fire yet!"

Jorgy nodded and sighted down his machine gun toward the opposite side of the airport. Matt called Wells and told him to sit tight. Then Oby came across the net.

"Heads up, guys! Straight across, the hangar on the right. The one without a front door. Check out the small office to the right, painted gray, you've got five riflemen on the ground. They are on the southern side of the hangar back in the shadows!"

Matt heard Jorgy respond to Oby's report over the net with a roger and then open up with his M-60. The big gun blasted the enemy position. The weapon's 7.62 NATO round was designed to travel eleven hundred meters. Jorgy was tearing the enemy apart from a distance of only two hundred meters. Matt's first reaction was to stop Jorgy, but then it dawned on him that this is what his men were trained to do.

Oby and Jorgy were eliminating the enemy squad by coordinating their fires, and they didn't need an officer to tell them how to do it! Matt stayed on his belly and crawled over to Chief Auger. The chief had his face pressed against his rifle. He was focusing his laser aim point, taking care to make every bullet count. The chief saw Matt next to him and passed him small M-911 night vision scope.

"LT! Look to the north! I think I saw movement over there."

Matt grabbed the scope and looked where the chief had pointed. There were more Egyptian troops between the hangars firing at the SEALs. Matt shouted, "Chief! You were right!"

Matt slid the monocular device over to the chief and then reached over to grab Cruise by the leg.

"What's up, LT?" Cruise shouted, trying to be heard above Jorgy's pounding.

"Direct your grenade launcher on those guys to the north! Use high explosive rounds!"

Cruise didn't need to reply. He smoothly jacked the cannister round out of the M-203 grenade launcher and popped in a killer egg. Bloop! The HE round traveled in a high lazy arch. It landed squarely in the middle of the enemy squad with a loud CRUMP! The second round fired by Cruise was in the air already. He again scored a direct hit. The firing from that location ended abruptly.

Matt winked at Cruise then checked his watch. Eight minutes to go! He looked up at the brightening morning sky and pressed the transmission button on his throat mike.

"Wells!"

Wells came back immediately. "Hey, LT, what the hell's going on up there?"

Matt decided not to relay all the dirty details. "Look, Wells, I need you to contact the incoming air support assets and tell them we are under heavy attack from the eastern side of the airport. Tell them to get here fast and hit anything that moves, on the eastern side of the runway!"

"You got it, boss!" Wells answered. "I'm on it!"

The plan required marking their position with green smoke to avoid being shot by their own fire support. Matt fingered the smoke grenade secured to his h-harness to confirm its presence. When the time came he would toss the grenade out on the apron in front of them. It just might act as a sufficient smoke screen to cover their withdrawal through the back of the hangar.

Banadar and his hand picked team drove to the northern tip of the airport and crossed the runway. He directed the small convoy to pull over and park a few hundred meters short of the American position. He was going to approach the enemy on foot. Once close enough to attack, he would swing his soldiers out onto the runway like a door slamming shut on the hangar concealing the invaders. The other troops deployed across the way had performed their part well.

The Americans were so focused on the two squads opposite them; they were totally unaware of Banadar's presence nearby. Banadar had radio communication with the two decoy squads and he told them now to shift fire to the south when they saw Banadar's men execute the trap door maneuver. He was about to signal his men to move when a loud explosion startled him.

Even with Matt's ears covered, the sound of the AT-4 antitank rocket was deafening. Chief Auger discarded the rocket tube and smiled at Matt. "I just got tired of messing around, LT! I doubt those suckers will poke their heads up again!"

"I'm sure that shook them up a bit!" Matt replied. Cruise was shook up too. The chief had forgotten to warn his partner that he was firing the rocket launcher. Within seconds after the rocket attack, the fire from directly across the SEALs position weakly continued. It was clear the Egyptians' heart wasn't in it.

Oby called in and told Matt he thought the fire had shifted south. "Oh, by the way boss, "he continued. "There's more company arriving near the tower."

Matt was still trying to figure out why the Egyptians would shift fire to the south when the boom of Oby's rifle shook the tin hangar again.

"Scratch one truck!" Oby reported.

Just then a torrent of lead slammed into the hangar walls. Jorgy screamed, "I'm hit!"

The chief jumped up when he heard the scream. He was almost on top of Jorgy when Chief Auger flipped into the air, twisting grotesquely in mid-flight. The body landed in a crumbled pile next to Jorgy. Cruise was shouting and firing frantically.

A bullet had passed through Jorgy's right hand and shattered his weapon's pistol grip. He shifted his left hand to what was left of the firing mechanism and opened fire. Cruise was firing at soldiers swinging around the north end of the hangar at close range.

Matt swiveled and fired at the same time. He hit a man coming around the corner near Cruise's prone figure. Cruise rolled onto his back and added five more rounds into the surprised soldier. Matt now had time to check out the chief.

"Doc!" Matt screamed. The chief had taken a direct hit in the chest. He was making a loud gurgling noise. Matt stared at the growing pool of blood on the hangar floor under the chief's body. Doc burst through the rear door just in time to shoot another Egyptian drawing a bead on Matt. He dove to the floor near the chief and grabbed the man's combat vest. He started dragging and sliding the chief back toward the rear of the building. It was always a bad idea to treat a man in the middle of a live firefight.

Doc got the wounded man to the back door where Wells helped pull them both out of the line of fire. Matt wanted to help the chief but he knew Doc could take care of it. If they stayed there much longer, Matt realized, his team would be cut to ribbons. The platoon leader glanced at his watch for the tenth time. Where are the Rangers?

As if on cue, Matt could hear the sound of heavy small arms exchange near the northern end of the runway. A helicopter gunship screamed overhead belching death in the form of twenty-millimeter electric cannons.

"Boss!" Wells voice cut through all the noise in Matt's ear.

"Boss, throw the damn smoke!"

Matt struggled to dislodge the smoke grenade attached to his vest. Banadar screamed at his men to pull back. The stupid farm boys had executed poorly. Only a few had actually moved out in front of the hangar opening. Of these, four were still laying where they fell. He could hear the loud explosions and firing to the north, it was the American main-force action. It had to be!

Banadar was starting to have second thoughts about staying. Maybe it was best to leave this place before it was too late!

Matt strained to see the approaching aircraft. As soon as he saw a helicopter, he was going to pump smoke and get his men out. Cruise had shifted position so he was next to Jorgy and the big gun.

"Hey boss!" Matt could hear the alarm in Oby's voice over the radio circuit.

"Go ahead!" Matt answered.

"LT, I'm running real low on fifty-caliber ammo and the tower area is swarming with bad guys. I don't think I can do much good up here anymore. Request permission for me and Boone to join you guys."

Matt thought about the request for a moment. It definitely was time to circle the wagons and get off the target. "Sure thing, Oby!" Matt agreed. "Come around the front of the hangar and yell when you're here."

Matt stood up and ran over to tell Jorgy and Cruise what was going on when he was hit hard by a sledgehammer in the leg and went down. Boone and Oby ran around the hangar wall just as a second blast of twenty millimeter shredded the Egyptians on the other side of the runway.

Another gunship was pounding the assembled reinforcements next to the tower. Oby and Boone threw themselves flat as a PAVLOW screamed by directly overhead. Boone popped a green smoke and rolled it onto the taxiway. He could see his platoon officer rolling around on the floor near Cruise. Matt struggled to regain his feet. Wells' voice cut through the chaos.

"Rangers on the ground, Rangers on the ground!"

Banadar could see the large wedge shaped formation of Rangers spreading out over the northern end of the airport. The American helicopters were deploying hundreds more to the west, just beyond the security fence. The only way out now was south past the American reconnaissance team. The firing from the hangar had died off completely possibly indicating the small unit had moved or succumbed to the Egyptian attack. Banadar gathered his men about him and gave them their new instructions.

Behind the hangar Doc was working frantically to save the chief 's life. Wells had already alerted the MEDEVAC unit that the SEALs had a critically wounded man. Doc overheard Boone tell Wells that the LT was hit.

Boone and Oby crossed the last five yards of open space and threw themselves down next to Matt. The hangar was flooding with light from the sun rising over the raging combat.

"Hang in there, LT!" Boone shouted as he started treating Matt's ugly thigh wound.

"What's the picture out there?" Matt asked through clenched teeth.

"The Rangers are halfway up the runway and the air force trashed the goons across the runway."

Matt pointed to the north side of the hangar. "Oby, tell everyone to fall back on Wells and Doc. I want you to protect the group from over there. I think those guys that attacked us are getting squeezed between us and the Rangers!"

"You got it, LT!" Oby responded. "Well you heard the man! Grab him and get the hell out of here!"

Boone and Cruise lifted Matt to his feet and helped him to the back of the hangar. They joined the rear security element and laid Matt down right next to the chief. Matt turned his head to look at his second in command. The gurgling sound coming out of his mouth gave Matt a sinking feeling.

The chief was struggling for his life. He'd been hit in the lungs and that wasn't good. Doc knew his stuff, but out here he wouldn't be able to do much for a collapsed lung. Matt rose up on his elbows to get a last head count.

"Where's Oby?" he asked Wells.

CHAPTER SIXTEEN

Banadar could hear the firefights all around them as the Rangers cleaned out the Egyptians one hangar at a time. His plan was simple. He would move south behind a wall of soldiers, sticking tightly to the hangars on the west side of the runway. Once clear of the airport he would return to Cairo and organize the Egyptian counterattack. The Americans may have secured an airport, but conquering Egypt was another thing together. This land had swallowed up invading armies for centuries. This was only a minor setback. They would be avenged!

The sergeant standing next to Banadar tried to get his master's attention. Muttering something to him, interrupting his thoughts. "What? What red dot, you imbecile?"

The sergeant pointed at Banadar's forehead. Oby squeezed the trigger of his MP-5SD, and saw with satisfaction that his aim had once again been true. The loud man giving all the commands to the Egyptian soldiers flipped violently backwards and then laid still, a small hole in his head oozing blood. Just another officer, Oby thought. Maybe the others will disperse now.

Banadar's eyes stared blankly at the dawn sky. He couldn't hear the sound of his men throwing their weapons down. He didn't see them tearing off their uniforms and running in terror from the approaching Americans.

Oby heard the sound of a C-130 cargo plane making its approach. He turned and jogged to the back of the hangar to rejoin the rest of his platoon. The final three air force PAVLOWs flew in a staggered column formation. Flying only four feet above the tarmac, they headed south, landing near the control tower to deploy more Rangers.

Oby was standing over Matt trying to tell him something about a great headshot. Matt couldn't focus. He knew that he'd lost a lot of blood and he was beginning to drift in and out. His fatigued mind began to wander, back to a time when only one thing mattered in life. Capturing the love and respect of a rugged old marine. Matt could still hear Oby chattering, but it seemed like he was a million miles away.

Matt could barely see through the mental fog. There seemed to be new faces around him. Army medics were working on the chief and attending to Matt's swollen leg. A Ranger squad was deployed around the SEAL platoon providing security behind the hangar.

Matt drifted back into consciousness when the medic started the IV in his arm. The army medics began the process of stabilizing Chief Auger for the flight back to the carrier.

Doc saw Matt looking at the chief. He leaned over Matt.

"He's going to make it, LT! The chief is going to pull through!"

The Rangers moved the SEALs to the runway in preparation for the MEDEVAC helicopter. To Matt's right, Chief Auger had just regained consciousness. The medic told the chief he had lost a lot of blood but he'd be okay.

As the sound of the incoming MEDEVAC helicopter began build, Matt looked over at the chief and yelled.

"Well chief, we did it!"

The chief looked at Matt and nodded his head gently. "No boss, you did it! And you're bringing all our guys home." Chief Auger reached out to Matt, gripping his hand. "Any time, anywhere, LT!"

Matt squeezed his chief's outstretched hand, tears welling up in his eyes. He rotated his head so he could see the blue desert sky above the target. Did you hear that, Dad? Top that, you old bastard!

EPILOGUE

The American and NATO forces assigned to Operation Sparrow Hawk continued to pour into Egypt through multiple ports of entry. As the word spread of Banadar's death, the rebel military leadership who supported him and his cause came forward, prepared to swear allegiance to the new provisional government.

In Washington, D.C., the Chairman of the Joint Chiefs of Staff sat at his desk pondering the off-white personnel folder. The folder contained background information on Lt. Matthew Barrett, United States Navy. The chairman knew intuitively that critical events in warfare often hinged on the actions of a few. It always seemed to come down to one good man leading other good men for a cause they believe in, a man like this young navy SEAL. A man who could pull off the Alexandria airport mission could be very useful in the future.

The Chairman slid the file off to his left and made a mental note to make sure that

Lt. Barrett's career was monitored very closely from now on.

ABOUT THE AUTHOR

Martin L. Strong is a retired Navy SEAL and a veteran of over thirty special operations combat missions. He is president of Special Operations Solutions, a leadership consulting firm. *Death Before Dawn* is the first novel in the SEAL Strike trilogy featuring SEAL Lieutenant Matthew Barrett. Watch for his new installment–*The Warrior Code*, due in bookstores May 2003. More information can be found by visiting www.sealstrike.com

0-595-18454-5

Printed in the United States
1490700005B/83